CHICAGO JAZZ

CHICAGO
JAZZ

GREGORY C. RANDALL

Printed in the United States of America

Windsor Hill Publishing, Inc.
Walnut Creek, California 94596

ISBN: 978-0-9908872-7-0

This story is dedicated to
my grandmothers,
Eva Struble and Beatrice Smith

1

LIMESTONE STEPS climbed from the street to the narrow brick front of the West Side Chicago speakeasy. Every window had its shades lowered. In the dim glow of the cranberry-glass oil lamps that lit the rooms within, the shadows of the men and women inside appeared grotesque, flickering ghostlike behind translucent curtains, their individual sexes all but indistinguishable. The moans of a reedy tenor saxophone leaked out through a second-floor window, cracked an inch to keep out the late-June heat wave. Along with the jazz-infused sounds came a thick and sweet cigarette-opiate fog.

A yellow taxi slid to a stop at the base of the steps to the tenement. First to leave the cab from the rear passenger's seat was a tall, angular man, dressed in a lightweight tuxedo and black patent leather shoes. His eyes were hidden in the shadow of a black fedora with a wide satin band. His complexion, as much as could be seen, had faded to a gray-white, and the hair visible below the rim of his hat was cropped close to his head. His crisp, pencil-thin mustache was, like his nose, clipped sharp. All in all, his look favored a poor relation of the actor William Powell.

The man reached a black kid-gloved hand through the open car door and helped a lanky young woman exit. She might have been mistaken for his daughter. Her long alabaster-like legs, draped in sheer silk stockings, tentatively probed for the curb and then the filthy sidewalk. Once out of the car, she pulled a borrowed silk scarf close to her chin. Her faux diamond earrings and fitted jeweled cap sparkled in the pale light thrown from a cracked streetlight. Only the briefest wisps of her stylishly cut black hair escaped the cap.

Her companion paid the driver through the window, took the girl firmly by the arm, and escorted her up the limestone steps to the paneled oak door, framed by two rose-colored glass sconces. The young woman glanced nervously back at the street and the fleeing taxi and then turned and watched as her escort pressed a black button on the door. A series of buzzes could be heard through the open transom over the door. More billows of the sweet smog spilled from the tilted window like fog escaping over a mountain.

"You will love it, Miss DeAngelo," the gentleman whispered. "This is where the good times are. All the jazz folks and finer people come here."

She snuggled against his elegant tuxedo; she had never felt anything so soft.

"This is so exciting and so debonair, Mr. Jamison.

The door opened. A wasp-like woman in a semiopaque black dress stood silhouetted in the hallway light. A cigarette holder, limply held, balanced an inch of ash on the cigarette's tip, waiting for the right moment to fall.

"Why, Mr. Jamison, welcome," the sallow woman lisped. "This is an unexpected but delightful surprise. And you brought a friend. How fun will this be. Please come in, my dear. You may leave your wraps to the left with Charlotte. Cold drinks are to the right—you know the arrangements, Mr. Jamison. Please show the lady around. We are here for your pleasure."

"Thank you, Mai Lee. You are, as always, most accommodating," Mr. Jamison replied.

"Is she a China woman? Is this your private club?" the young lady mewed softly in his ear.

She held tightly to Mr. Jamison's coat sleeve while he waved off Charlotte, to whom Miss DeAngelo paid little attention. It was the lush room, the Negro saxophone player, and his quartet, all Negros as well, that dazzled her.

"Mr. Jamison, it's like a Charlie Chan movie. The carpets and the wallpaper—it's so decadent," the girl said. "And so debonair."

She ran her hand over the ebony side table, mindless of the nicks and heavy scratches, the silks that covered the chairs stressed and thin from age. A worn ottoman, wrapped in a remnant of a Persian rug, sat off to one side. The parlor with its oriental decorations vaguely reminded the girl of a rich friend's house back in Milwaukee, Wisconsin; but then again no, no—definitely not. That would never have happened; her friends never would have allowed Negroes in their house except to cook and clean.

She stood breathing in the heady, sweet smell that hung like a gray haze over all the swells and their dates lounging about the parlor. In one corner of the room, a woman, dark-eyed with glossy black hair cropped tight to her head, sat alone on a red velvet settee. She held a glass of champagne and in her lap cradled a long pipe with a blackened cup secured to one end. The woman was a modern, tall and lanky, and a few, yet indeterminate, years older than Miss DeAngelo. She wore an elegant, mannish suit with a white satin shirt and thin black tie. The woman smiled and nodded at her. Embarrassed, the girl turned away, uncomfortable at feeling the woman's eyes follow her as she walked with Mr. Jamison to the combo, where he poured her a glass of clear green liqueur.

"You *must* have this, my dear. It tastes like licorice, an adult licorice, but be careful, it's a sophisticated and acquired taste," he said.

Mary Ann DeAngelo wished to be more sophisticated with each new day she spent in Chicago. She was so pleased that Mr. Jamison was taking the time to show her around the city. It was not like Milwaukee at all, or the home of her parents in Whitefish Bay. No, not at all.

"What is she doing, Mr. Jamison?" she asked.

He glanced in the direction she was pointing.

"She's smoking pen-yan, an herb from China. This house specializes in its use, and all of this is owned by our host, Mai Lin."

He looked down at Mary Ann.

"It will give you wonderful dreams," he said softly.

"It smells sweet," she said, half to herself.

She waggled her finger at Jamison, and he came closer.

"Is it like opium?" she whispered.

He smiled.

"Why yes, my dear, it is. Would you like to try a little?"

"Oh, I'm happy with this for now. Maybe later, but this is all so wicked. I'll wait and see."

"That's all I ask my dear, that's all I ask," Mr. Jamison said, in his most fatherly voice, the voice he frequently used with his wife and children at home in Kansas.

He gently touched Mary Ann's arm.

"I have some business with Mai Lin, my dear. Why don't you go sit with that young woman; she looks attracted to you. I'll be right back."

Left alone in the center of the parlor, Mary Ann rocked on her heels. A breezy tune from the black sax player almost made her move her slim hips under her fancy dress—the borrowed garment was the color of old ivory. She pirouetted about on the borrowed white shoes; the shoes matched the fashionable belt secured two inches above her thin midriff, giving support to her modest bodice. The other girls in the room were all more amply endowed, their attire displaying the soft crowns of their breasts, causing her to wish that hers were fuller.

The woman in the corner smiled at her again and patted the red velvet cushion next to her.

Mary Ann returned the smile and as confidently as she could, walked across the oriental carpet to where the woman waited.

When she stood, the modern woman was, at least, a foot taller than Mary Ann. Extending her hand, she said, "I'm Carla Acerbi. I believe *you* can call me Carla. You look like a fucking virgin canary in a coal mine."

Shocked by the crude remark, Mary Ann nonetheless lowered herself onto the settee and, as she did so, slowly ran her small left hand over her bottom, straightening the silky fabric of her dress; her right hand still held the glass of green liqueur. When settled, her hands clasped in her lap, the tall glass with its wide base tightly wedged between her fingers, she said carefully, "What an elegant room."

"There are better, especially in Venice. In fact, this is a bit of a dump if you asked me, but the smoke is cheaper here; so here I am. Is that old man your father? Sure as hell could be."

The woman's accent was hard to place. American for sure, but there was a subtlety to it that reminded Mary Ann of the way her grandfather had sounded when he was alive. It was the accent of an Italian immigrant.

"That's none of your business," she said aloud. "He's my date. He works in the building where I'm a secretary. It's in the Loop."

"In the Loop, I see," Acerbi said, taking a small mouthful of smoke from her pipe. "Care for some?"

"I heard it was evil?"

"Lots of stuff is evil. So is booze, but that doesn't stop people from drinking, so if not . . ."

"Maybe a small one, just to taste it. This is a night for new experiences, and this is just one more," Mary Ann offered.

"Put that on the table"—the woman gestured at the glass of absinthe Mary Ann still held—"and I'll show you."

Mary Ann did as asked and turned toward Acerbi, who extended the mouthpiece to her.

"Hold the pipe to your lips, no need to clench it with your teeth. When I nod my head, take a very small breath, don't suck."

The younger woman placed the end of the pipe against her lips, and Acerbi rotated the bowl over the lamp and nodded. Mary Ann smiled against the pipe's end, nodded and inhaled. She immediately felt as if her eyes might explode. She started to cough and almost retched; the coughing continued. The black bassist noticed and chuckled, and the sax player wailed a long note that ended in a reedy laugh.

Mary Ann didn't think it was at all funny.

"That stuff is awful—worse than the time I tried a cigarette. No wonder it's illegal."

"Oh, you can get used to it, but that's enough for now. I see your old man is returning," Carla said, sounding amused. She inclined her head toward where Mr. Jamison was exiting a room off the hallway.

"My *father* lives in Milwaukee with my mother," Mary Ann said stiffly.

Acerbi watched Jamison discreetly adjust the waistband of his formal pants and reset his suspenders.

"Ah, Milwaukee, why am I not surprised," she said, not missing the slight swelling in his pants as Jamison casually crossed the carpet.

He retrieved a cigarette from a gold case and lit it with a gold lighter. "My dear, I must show you something upstairs," he said to Mary Ann, as he came up to where the two ladies sat. "This building is so elegant, you just have to see everything. And you must have more of the Green Goddess; it's such a special liqueur."

Looking past his shoulder, Acerbi watched Mai Lin slip back into the room from which Jamison had entered; there was slight damage to her makeup and a bit of lingerie peeked out over her slight bodice. Acerbi let out a low and derisive laugh.

Jamison ignored her and picked up Mary Ann's glass, then waved at an attendant. The waiter, a dwarf, hunched-back and misshapen, brought the bottle and expertly refilled the glass.

"Now you must take a long full sip to fully appreciate what the French have done with this wonderful liqueur," Jamison instructed his young charge.

"Oh, brother," Acerbi said under her breath.

Mary Ann looked sharply at Acerbi, then stood to accept the proffered glass. In one sweep of her hand she took up the glass and sipped, then emptied it in one long swallow. She set the glass down and abruptly placed her hand on the table for some needed stability.

"Now wasn't that just debonair, my dear? Just debonair?" Jamison said.

DeAngelo rocked a bit on her white pumps but managed to say, "Yes, quite debonair."

"Now if you'll excuse us, I will show this young lady the rest of the house," Jamison said to Acerbi.

Acerbi looked at the girl.

"Are you all right?"

Mary Ann giggled.

"Come, my girl, you must see the rest of the house," insisted Jamison, taking the girl's hand.

Acerbi sat back and watched him lead Mary Ann to the hallway. She drained the rest of her champagne, still watching as they climbed the ornate stairs and disappeared beyond the railing that wrapped the landing.

The quartet launched into an improvised version of Duke Ellington's current hit "Sophisticated Lady." Acerbi had to acknowledge that they were quite good, especially the sax man and the bassist. They finished the Ellington piece and had just started Eddy Duchin's "Night and Day" when an ear-shattering scream came from upstairs. The band froze. Acerbi bolted to the stairs, taking them three at a time, and when another scream cut the sudden silence, she knew which room. She threw her shoulder against the thin wood door; it exploded inward.

Mary Ann was lying on the bed, one small breast exposed, her underthings jumbled around her knees. Jamison, in his boxer shorts and gartered socks, glared at Acerbi.

"What the fuck are you doing, you bitch?" Jamison said, obviously not the gentleman he impersonated.

He grabbed something shiny off the dresser; it was a switchblade, which he flicked open.

"This ain't your fucking business. Get the hell out of here." He waved the knife.

Carla Acerbi smiled, grabbed a cushion from the chair near the door and flung it at Jamison. The blade easily pierced the pillow, but the hasp caught on its gold fringe and Jamison, jerking the handle, couldn't dislodge the blade. In two strides, Acerbi crossed the room and grabbed Jamison by the throat with her right hand, and ripped away the pillow with her left. With blinding speed, she released her hold on his throat and with her palm punched in the left side of his nose, knocking the fool to the cheap carpet. Blood poured from his broken nose; it spotted the carpet with his every painful heave. Acerbi expertly gathered the girl's things, cupped the girl under her left arm and swaddled her with a sheet she jerked from the bed. She could tell that Mary Ann was generally unharmed, embarrassed, but unspoiled.

Jamison dragged himself vertical and lunged at Acerbi, trying to pull the girl away; Acerbi calmly kicked him in the groin. Jamison went down again. She kicked him in the head, further battering his nose; now it was twisted to the left. She picked up his tuxedo jacket, making sure not to bang the girl's head as they stepped through the shattered doorframe. Mai Lin appeared in the hallway, screaming at Acerbi in Chinese, then ran into the room and cradled the head of the bloody and now unconscious Mr. Jamison. Acerbi wrapped Jamison's fine black tuxedo coat around the half-naked girl and left the bed sheet draped over the edge of the half-door of the cloakroom. She dropped two dollars on the plate and headed out the door into the hot evening, the girl still in tow. She heard the bassist laughing as the door closed behind them. The sax man had begun to play "Stormy Weather."

Acerbi hailed a taxi. When the driver stopped, Acerbi helped the girl into the backseat and made sure the coat completely covered her.

"She all right, sir? I don't want some doper throwing up in my taxi," the cabbie said.

"I have a twenty here if you can keep your mouth shut," Acerbi said.

"Shut it is, shut it is. Sorry ma'am, didn't see you."

The girl whimpered like a small kitten, but it was more a demure moan than a purr. She opened her eyes and looked at Acerbi.

"He was going to force me to . . .," she whispered.

"He won't hurt you anymore. Where do you live?"

"I share an apartment on Rush Street at Oak."

"My place is quicker. You can rest there. I still have your twenty, cabbie."

"Address?" the driver asked.

"North State Street near North."

"Thank you," Mary Ann said. "He was so nice until he wasn't."

"The man's a cad. I should have crushed his face so no one would want him. But you did get a reward; that coat's worth maybe a cool two hundred, if a dime."

"You keep it as a prize," Mary Ann told her. "It's my reward to you."

The cab bounced and roared over the iron grating of the Michigan Avenue Bridge that spanned the Chicago River. Neither woman said anything as the driver continued north.

"What's your name?" Acerbi eventually asked.

She tenderly moved a strand of black hair away from the girl's eye.

"Mary Ann. Mary Ann DeAngelo, and I remember yours—Carli Acerba."

"Good enough, Mary Ann DeAngelo, good enough," Acerbi said, putting one arm around the girl to draw her close.

2

THE CALL HAD COME in to the Racine Station at
first light. A contractor excavating a foundation for a new
building at the corner of Lake and Peoria had reported the
discovery.

"There's a body in my hole," the man had said, his accent
thick and Eastern European.

"You sure?" McDunnah had asked.

The desk sergeant had been on the job long enough to
regard such calls as a matter of course.

"I fought in the war. I's know what a fuck'n dead body
looks like."

"Okay, okay. I'll send a prowler."

So now here was Chicago Detective Tony Alfano, whose
shoes were going to be soaking wet and very muddy in a matter of minutes, standing at the edge of the sidewalk, looking
over a wooden barricade into a forty-foot-deep construction
pit. He hunched his trench coat higher up on his shoulders,
turned the lapels and watched the rain drip off the brim of his
gray fedora.

At the bottom of the crater, a burly man hunkered next
to a couple uniforms; the large man, the coroner, waved for
Alfano to come down. The detective looked at his watch, then

back at the hole. The water was already a foot deep in the far corner; the body's feet were submerged.

"Fuck," was all that Alfano could mutter, as he headed for the dirt ramp that sloped down into the pit. It had already been two hours since the call on this early Saturday morning; two hours for the rain to wash everything clean and shiny, sluice away evidence, and make the ramp as slippery as the proverbial road to hell. If he made it without getting mud all over his already wet clothes, he would declare it a pyrrhic victory.

"Isn't this a lot of fun," Alfano said, when he got to the bottom.

"Like a fucking picnic it is, a fucking family picnic," the coroner said.

Alfano extracted a pack of Lucky Strikes from his inside coat pocket; one of the uniforms produced a lighter and lit the cigarette.

"Thanks, Jimmy," Alfano said, regarding the remains of a young woman; her body lay facedown. His practiced glance took in the obvious details: white, young, nice legs, and young, too young. The rain-soaked thin white dress revealed the lack of underwear. He couldn't tell if she wore shoes since her feet were under water.

"What do we have?" he asked the coroner.

"From the bruising on the back of the neck, it looks like she was strangled with a thin rope or scarf—that's just a guess. Found this protruding out from under her."

He held up a mud-soaked white rope, water dripping off its end.

"I don't think it happened here," he told Alfano. "The girl may have been dumped. But with all this mud and rain, hard to tell."

"Time?"

"She's still in rigor, so right now I'd say during the last eight to twelve hours."

"How do you think she got here?" Tony asked him.

"That's your job, not mine. The rain started about three a.m.. Someone might have driven down the ramp and discarded the body before that."

"Certainly not trying to hide her, were they?"

"Guess not. I'm rolling her. Jimmy, can you give me a hand?"

"Yes, sir," the patrolman answered, and the two men deftly flipped the girl onto her back. Everyone sucked in a breath; the second cop turned away and heaved up his breakfast.

"Jesus H. Christ," Alfano said quietly.

The girl's face was crushed and mangled, like it had been used as a punching bag. The eyes were puffy and closed tightly. One ear, partially hidden by her hair, was torn, the nose twisted, the lips swollen, and the open mouth showed three front teeth were gone. The rain continued to wash away the mud, revealing facial bruises and a cut above the left eye. The left cheek had what looked to Alfano like a burn mark.

"Saw this when Capone's gangs were pushing into new territories," the coroner said, "but never to a woman."

He pointed at the cheek.

"That's maybe from a blowtorch. Shit, they really messed this girl up. Look at her hands, Detective; every finger is bent and crushed. I'll know more after the autopsy. Need anything else, Detective?"

Alfano continued to look at the dead girl. Something else about the body was just not right; maybe it was the clothes, maybe the wet haircut.

"Detective?"

"No, nothing more. How soon can you do the autopsy?"

"Surprisingly, it has been quiet. Nobody waiting, so maybe this afternoon."

Something about this was distinctive. Alfano couldn't see it yet, but it was peculiar. He'd seen too many murder victims over his twenty odd years, and this one was . . . different.

"Can you get fingerprints?" he asked.

"As soon as I get her back to the morgue. It's impossible here," came the reply.

"GOOD MORNING, DETECTIVE. HAVING FUN YET?" Sergeant McDunnah said, as Alfano came into the Racine Street Station. Water dripped from his overcoat, leaving spots on the lobby's dusty tile floor.

"You are the second person this morning to ask. I hate dead bodies in the morning, and especially in the rain."

"Wasn't his fault—I'm sure. Coffee?"

"It was a her not a him. Yes, coffee."

Tony stripped away his wet coat and shook the water off his hat before pushing his way through the swinging gates into the detectives' bullpen of the station. As he reached his desk, McDunnah set down a large mug of coffee.

"Her? That's different. We don't get too many of those," McDunnah remarked. "Donuts?"

"Watching my waist."

"Like hell. You ate three the other day."

"That was the other day, before my wonderful two days off. Today my diet begins."

"Jesus, Mary and Joseph, Detective. You say that the first of every month."

"This time, I mean it."

"You say that too. What did you find?"

Alfano took a sip of his coffee. Something odd about the dead girl still nagged at him.

"Do you think this was done by the mob—a girl that crossed someone in the wrong way?" McDunnah asked, after Alfano had finished going over what he and the coroner found in the hole. The torture and beating had a similar M.O. to what they'd seen seven and eight years ago, McDunnah reminded him.

"You remember the guy they called the Blow Torch?" the sergeant said. "He used one of those just for fun before he killed his victim."

Alfano nodded, took a few more sips of coffee.

"Yeah, thought of that. This hot weather made the idea of a blow torch jump right into my mind. However, there was something different about this. Her hands were broken, then the beating. It escalated; this poor girl was being tortured for some reason, and it got worse as it went on."

The phone rang at the sergeant's desk. McDunnah casually walked to the front of the squad room and answered. It was the coroner's office, calling for Alfano. McDunnah waved at Tony, who picked up the phone at his desk. For a few minutes the detective scribbled in his notebook and then hung up.

"Seems that our dead girl may be from the near North Side," he told McDunnah. "She matches the description of a girl who didn't come home last night."

The girl's roommates had called police and were now on the way to the morgue to identify her—"If she's the one," Alfano added.

"Damn shame," McDunnah said. "What else?"

"The coroner Abrahamson says after his cursory exam that there isn't evidence of sexual attack, but there was significant damage and bruising in that area. Someone was very angry."

3

THE RAIN during the previous night dialed down a few degrees the heat that had hung over Chicago since early June. As he drove the Packard to the morgue, Alfano watched people walking in the rain, just because they could. No one complained about the rain, and he thought that if someone did, no one would pay attention. Then again, they hadn't found a tortured young woman in a deep hole in the ground before Saturday breakfast.

He stood off to one side of the hallway as the coroner's assistant escorted two young women down the corridor. Both were about twenty, give or take a year or two, and stylishly dressed in long, thin skirts and gauzy light blouses. Their shoes were polished but surprisingly practical. Both women wore cloth caps, topped with a bright band and bow. Alfano never understood the need to have the latest fashion; the women looked like the models found in magazines like *Screen* or *Cosmopolitan*. They disappeared through the swinging double doors that led to the morgue. Thirty seconds later, they came out sobbing and holding tightly to each other. Alfano stopped them in the hallway.

"Was that your roommate?" he asked, not introducing himself.

The taller of the two, a brunette with slick red lipstick, looked at Alfano and took a deep, heaving breath.

"Yes. It kind of looks like her, she looks awful. We almost couldn't tell who it was. She borrowed my earrings, that's how I knew. What happened?"

"That's what I'm trying to find out. When did you last see her?"

The other girl, a redhead with a bright Irish look about her, said that she'd seen her friend yesterday afternoon.

"I had the day off. She was getting ready for a date."

"With whom? And what's your name?"

"Lily. Lily O'Leary."

Their girlfriend had refused to say who the date was—"Very hush-hush about it," Lily told Alfano tearfully. "She had only been in town for about a month, and this was her first date. Our guess, someone from work." Lilly quickly glanced at her friend.

"You didn't work with her?" Alfano asked.

"We work at Marshall Field's on State. She's a secretary somewhere on Wacker; don't know where," the brunette said.

"She's your roommate, and you don't know?" Alfano said.

He asked the brunette's name.

"Sally Spiegel, sir. She was recommended through one of those rental agencies. She seemed like a good kid, a little naïve but pleasant. Made more than us, so we were good. She paid three months in advance. The landlord was pleased."

"What's his name?"

"He's a woman—Mrs. Jones. No first name I know," answered Sally.

Lily nodded her agreement.

"She owns the building," Lily said. "We heard something about a dead husband and the war. She's nice enough for an old lady but has rules about dates. No one can come up to the apartment. Mrs. Jones wants no fooling around on her property."

"Fooling around?"

Lily blushed.

"You know what I mean. We girls just have to have some fun. So Mary Ann leaves on her date in a cab. She borrowed my jeweled cap—hey, did they find it?"

"No cap. Nothing, not even a coat," Alfano told Lily.

"Mary Ann DeAngelo," the redhead said, when he asked the victim's name. "She was from somewhere near Milwaukee—the name had a fish in it or something. Anyway, she took the train home last weekend to see her folks. She seemed pretty happy when she got back."

"That's right," said Alice. "Something about her family."

"As we said, pleasant enough girl, for an Italian," Lily said.

"I'm Italian, young lady."

"Sorry, didn't mean anything. Just saying that's what she was. She never stayed out late; that's what got us nervous. It wasn't in her nature . . . . Who would do that to her?"

"Nature?"

"Pure and virginal-like," Lily said. "She didn't drink, went to Holy Name Cathedral, read a lot, punctual—"

"Do you think it was her date?" Alice wanted to know.

"Don't know"—Alfano handed each of them a card—"If you think of anything, call the number and the tell the sergeant who answers. If I'm not there, I'll get back to you."

Both the girls seemed relieved after Alfano took down their information and address.

"We need to talk," the coroner said, when the young women had departed and Alfano stepped into the morgue.

The girl's beaten face was all that was exposed. A white sheet covered the rest of the body, affording some dignity to the remains. The eyes were still open but had lost their brightness. The mud had been washed away; the girl's short hair was plastered tightly to her skull from the rinse. Alfano turned away, it was hard to look at Mary Ann's face, a face that was once pretty, once being just twenty-four hours earlier.

"What do you have?" he asked Dr. Abrahamson.

"Like I said, I didn't find any evidence of coitus, no semen, nothing that would signify sexual relations. But there was damage and bruising. Death was from asphyxiation, most probably strangulation. It could be the rope we found at the scene"—the coroner motioned for Alfano to follow him to a corner of the room—"but you have to see this," he said.

Arranged on the coroner's marble countertop were two porcelain trays. The tray on the left held a neatly coiled white rope. In the other tray, a strip of fabric floated in a couple inches of water.

"This is the rope found in the pit?" Alfano said.

"Yes, but it's the other thing that's a little unnerving. I've never seen anything like it."

The 'thing' was a scarf, thin, about two feet long. Alfano used the coroner's tongs to carefully lift the fabric from the tray of water.

"That isn't something you see every day," he said, looking at the pattern printed on the silken fabric. "Where did you find it?"

"Inside her vagina, tightly rolled and deeply inserted."

"*Fasces*," Alfano said softly.

"You know what those symbols mean?"

Alfano nodded. Like any well-schooled Italian, he knew tradition and theater.

"It's an ancient Roman symbol for *imperium* or authority. A bundle of rods with an ax protruding, it goes back two thousand years to Roman times. Mussolini now uses it as a symbol for his fascists; in fact, the name comes from the root *fasces*. But what the hell is it doing here . . . in the privates of a young girl from Milwaukee?"

"That's for you to find out. Me, there's some more work I

need to do. The injuries are methodical and seem to escalate from the hands and legs to the face—there's something very strange about them. I'll know more after I do some additional tests and check her stomach contents. Maybe what she ate can tell us more."

"When you are done with that," Alfano pointed to the cloth in the tray, "can you dry it and get to me? Maybe I can find out where it came from."

"As far as I'm concerned, it came from hell."

THE RAIN had stopped when Alfano left the morgue and began his walk to the car. The cool air was a needed relief; everything including the scorched trees seemed thankful to suck in the moisture. Now covered in rainwater, they seemed freshened. Yet the respite was temporary; Alfano could feel the sun's heat pushing through the trees. When he turned the corner of the building, he almost ran into the two roommates. They stood with their backs to him, smoking cigarettes.

". . . told you that the old man was a bastard," Alfano heard one of them say.

"What old man?" he demanded.

Both girls spun toward him, reflexively throwing their cigarettes to the pavement.

"Nothing, it was nothing," Sally said, her voice too animated.

"Sounds like it was a lot more than nothing."

"It was nothing, just that, nothing," Lily insisted.

"My car is right there," Alfano said. "Why don't you two accompany me down to the station and we can discuss this in greater detail. Miss DeAngelo was brutally murdered, and you now mention an old man. So, what will it be, young ladies? Conversation here or interrogation at the station?"

"Detective Alfano, we both have to be to work at two

o'clock, or we'll lose our jobs. Our boss wouldn't understand at all about the police. Not at all," Sally said.

She took a couple steps away from him and into the sparse shade of a street tree.

"Spill it, girls," Alfano said.

Sally lit another cigarette.

"Well, there's this guy, old man really, maybe in his forties, who dates a lot of the girls in his office building. Least that's what Mary Ann said."

She glanced at Lily, who nodded.

"He is really nice to the girls and gives them things and shows them a good time and a dinner and drinks and all that," Sally went on. "He comes to town once or twice a month and shows the girls a good time."

"You said that—a good time. Where?"

"That, we don't know. Most of the girls, according to Mary Ann, just say they had a good time, that he was a debonair gentleman."

"Where did she work?"

"As I said, somewhere on Wacker. I don't know, really," Alice said. "She might have something in her room. I can check when we get back this evening."

She gave him a pleading look.

"Sir, we really have to go to work or we'll get fired."

Alfano thought for a minute about taking the girls in and getting more, but he also knew how hard it was to get a job, let alone hold onto one.

"I need to see her room. Does anybody else live with you two?"

"No, just us now," Lily told him.

She turned to her friend.

"Sally, we need to find another roommate. We can't afford the place without a roommate."

Alfano handed a second card—this one had his home

phone number printed on it—to redheaded Lily O'Leary.

"Call me this evening. Don't change or move anything in her room. If you do, I'll throw you both in jail—and don't tell your landlord either. I want to stop by in the morning and take a look. What time will you be home from church?"

The two looked at each other and smiled.

"Okay, when would it be convenient? Is ten o'clock too early? If I don't hear from you, I will come down to Marshall Field's Monday morning and interview you there."

"Oh, please don't do that. We'll call you this evening," Lily promised. "There's a pay phone in the hallway."

"Reverse the charges. I'll take it. You two need a lift?"

The girls looked at each like they had just made a pact with the devil.

"That would be just great. It's not a police car is it?" Lily asked.

Alfano dropped the girls at the curb in front of the Marshall Field's store on State Street and watched as they walked quickly through the ornate columned entry and disappeared into the huge department store.

I'm almost forty-three years old, and they called DeAngelo's date an old man—shit.

He put the Packard in gear and pulled into the early Saturday afternoon State Street traffic.

4

ITALIAN FASCIST secret agent and assassin Carla Acerbi stood at the window of the third-floor North Avenue apartment that overlooked Chicago's Lincoln Park. Mussolini's government provided well for its agents. She had been a member of the party since she was twenty-one years old and for ten-years had, more than once, proved that she was not the simpleminded *donna* and plaything some of the thuggish Blackshirts thought her to be. She had followed her father in joining the fascists as soon as women were allowed and now, with Mussolini's friend Herr Hitler as chancellor of Germany, there was much to be done and to defend.

Her father owned a cheese shop in Forlì, a small town near Mussolini's birthplace, and was easily won over by 'Il Duce' and his promises for the future of Italy. Carla had felt proud to stand alongside her father, him in his new uniform, listening to the speeches of Il Duce. Italy would change. It would become the powerful force it had been before the war that stripped the country of its men, treasury, and honor. Il Duce would restore all of it.

Acerbi had discovered three important traits about herself during her training and initial assignments: She would not submit to the government's ideas that women should return to the roles of reproduction and motherhood; her skills were needed elsewhere. She also learned that men, as companions, did not interest her, and that killing left no scar or impression on her. She did as ordered and had been able to use her talents to great effect on those who chose to oppose her *Duce*.

Mary Ann DeAngelo had been a credible source of information. The girl had maintained, even during her torture and eventual garroting, that she did not know the names of the three men who had visited her father the previous month. All she knew was that they were Italians and somehow connected to her father.

"But he knows nothing!" DeAngelo had screamed as her fingers were crushed. "Nothing. He just gave them food, they talked, and then they were gone."

Acerbi knew differently. Three days earlier she'd visited DeAngelo's place of work and was able to quickly parse out the character of the 'gentleman,' Mr. Jamison. Acerbi had asked the right questions and, knowing the worst sides of people, gleaned what kind of man Jamison was. Over a cup of tea with one of DeAngelo's coworkers, the secretary confided what she knew about Jamison and where he usually took his dates. The secretary had become flustered and embarrassed, but in time Acerbi learned everything about the man. Pretending to rescue DeAngelo from Jamison had allowed her the opportunity to console and then question and eventually interrogate the young woman. It had been exciting for one of them.

It had been late Friday evening when Acerbi removed the body from the small storage space she'd rented, placed Mary Ann DeAngelo in the trunk, and then left her in the pit. After thoroughly checking the car for any incriminating evidence and discarding a tarp, she returned her automobile to the basement garage and had the attendant thoroughly clean and wax the vehicle.

Now, enjoying a cigarette with her morning tea, she looked

out over the stately park grounds. Her next stop would be a place called Whitefish Bay—wherever the hell that was.

TONY ALFANO pinned a coroner's photo of Miss DeAngelo taken by the coroner on the corkboard that stood, like a large portable blackboard, behind his desk. As he collected additional information and evidence, more items would be fastened to the board. In time, he'd hope the bits and pieces would help form a picture of the crime and its perpetrator. Most detectives he knew kept the bits and pieces of a crime in their heads, allowing them to stew and eventually come together. More often than not, such 'clues' got lost or muddled. Sergeant McDunnah had suggested the board; now Alfano had developed a system. McDunnah was the only other person allowed to add clues to the board.

"To call them clues, McDunnah, sounds awfully like Sherlock Holmes," Alfano had said during one investigation.

"Clues is what they are, Detective," McDunnah had answered. "And when we have enough of them, we may even find our motive and then possibly the criminal. A crime is a sequence of events; if we can get them in the right order, we can find the answer."

"Or the bad guy."

"Yes, Detective, or the bad guy."

In time, other detectives had followed Alfano's lead and were using similar systems, but Alfano continued to refine his. Even though he had more than twenty years on the force, a few of the old-timers chided him over his painstaking scientific methods. Alfano would just shrug.

"Any word from her family?" Alfano now asked McDunnah, as the sergeant set a mug of coffee on the detective's desk.

"Not yet, sir. Seems they don't answer their phone, and it's going to take one of Whitefish Bay's boys to go to the

DeAngelo home and tell them. And it being Sunday and all, the officer I talked to said it may be late in the day before they could spare someone."

"Christ, Sergeant. If my daughter were dead, I sure as hell would want to know."

"Me as well, but that's how they run things up in Milwaukee. He said he'd call as soon as the family has been notified."

"Tell him thanks from me—the bastard."

McDunnah returned to his desk at the front of the station, where he began to talk with a patrolman who had a man in a ragged suit and frayed hat in tow. After a few minutes, McDunnah called out to Alfano that it would be a good idea to come over.

"This bum says that he was sleeping off a bender near that hole in the ground at Lake Street, and the rain hadn't started," McDunnah said.

"I's could feel the electricity in the air. Even my hairs stood up on my arm," the fellow said. "I's could hear the rum-blum of God's bowling balls up there. They's was bouncing all around the buildings. I's always liked thunder and the flashing about of electricity. Makes a man feel alive and all charged up."

"And I assume you saw something?" Alfano asked.

"I's think so. Awfully dark it was with the thundering and flashing, but yeah, think so. Didn't pay it no mind then, fell asleep when the rain started. But I's had a nice dry spot that I's have to protect—and I's protect it too—you know, from the other guys."

"And . . ."

Alfano felt his impatience rising a bit.

"Well, when I's rose up yesterday morning, I's saw all the cars and po-leece. First thing I's did was hide—didn't want no trouble with the po-leece. When it got lighter, some of the po-leece started walking around the neighborhood. Me, I's still hide. Don't want no trouble."

"Yeah, I get it. Patrolman Toms, where'd you find this guy?" Alfano said, looking at the cop.

"I've seen him around. Harmless guy. Gets soup and food a few blocks from the crime scene at that soup kitchen on Lake. We were told to ask around, and he's what I came up with."

"And?"

"Tell him, Oscar," Toms said.

"Why's, I's ask? Nothing in it for old Oscar."

"Could throw him in a holding cell," McDunnah offered. "That might jar his memory."

"My guess, he'd like it," Alfano said. "Hell of a better place than he slept last night."

He looked at the bedraggled fellow.

"So, Oscar, what do you have to tell me?"

Oscar looked longingly toward the row of unoccupied cells at the back of the station. He took a forlorn breath.

"Tall dude, with a nice car, stopped at the top of the hole and then slowly backed down, backways like, then opened the trunk and pulled something out."

"You said it was dark," McDunnah said.

"It was the flashes—kinda like one of those movies done real slow. Flash, there he was near the car; flash, then at the trunk; flash, it was open. Then for a while, no flashes. Then a flash, and the car were almost out of the hole. Then gone."

"Why didn't you go and see what happened?" Alfano asked.

"It started to rain, and ol' Oscar here did not want to get wet. So's I's just set in my special spot and waited. Sometimes I could see a spot of white in the hole when there was a flash, but that was about it."

"I know I'm going to regret this," Alfano said, "but do you know what time it was?"

Oscar smiled.

"I's sure as hell do, sir. I's have a watch, you know, a damn good one that the railroad gave me when they threw me out on my ass. When was that?"

Alfano stared at the man. This was going to take a while.

"Yes, were three years ago on Armistice Day," Oscar said. "Left me at the Tulsa station, they's did. Bastards."

He reached into his pocket and brought out a long bright chain; at the end was a pocket watch.

"Nice watch," McDunnah said.

"Best thing I's own. Fact is, it's the only thing I's own. So's when the car pulled out of the hole I took out my timepiece, opened her up and, bamm-flash, I nearly dropped it—lucky I got the chain. But the hands said three thirty-five. It was like stuck on my eyeballs due to the thunder and flash. It was incinerated into my brain."

"I can believe that," Toms said.

Alfano smiled at Toms.

"Get this guy some breakfast and take him to the Salvation Army store. Tell Wanda there I said to get him a new suit, and burn the one he's wearing. Send the bill to me. She knows me."

"Yes, sir. Let's go, Oscar. This might be your lucky day."

"I's lucky every day, you betcha."

Alfano and McDunnah watched the two men leave the station.

"Ah, to be free of the cares of the world and as a lark, sing to the bright day," McDunnah said.

"Yeah, and you might look around for fleas and a few other nasties that might have fallen off that fellow," Alfano told him. "At least, we have a good call on the time the body was dumped."

He wrote *Saturday morning, June 24, 1933 - 3:35 a.m.* on an index card and stuck it on the board next to a photo the coroner had snapped of Mary Ann DeAngelo's lifeless body sprawled facedown in the hole.

5

ALFANO headed home with a paper bag full of articles he'd removed from Mary Ann DeAngelo's dresser and nightstand. He parked the Packard at the curb in front of his apartment building on Chicago's near North Side. The car belonged to the Chicago Police Department and had been recovered from a brewery bust. Alfano was neither fan nor aficionado of automobiles, but he did tolerate their convenience. His apartment was a few miles from the Racine Street Station. He'd thought about moving closer, but he liked the neighborhood and the nearby restaurants. He also liked the whiskey sold by one of the quiet speakeasies hidden at the back of a small pharmacy. The owner served good Canadian whiskey directly off the boat. What the fellow would do when Prohibition was finally lifted at the end of the year, Alfano wasn't sure. He hoped that the elderly mick had put away a few dollars in anticipation. The place would make a good bar; the man certainly had the customers. They'd never talked about it, but Alfano was sure that the mick knew he was a cop. But then again, he probably had a dozen other cops who were clients.

Alfano's apartment was up two flights of stairs. Along with the bag of evidence, he carried up a shopping bag full of vegetables and a half-pound of ground chuck under his arm as well as a roll of toilet paper and other personal sundries. At the landing, he glanced at Teddy and Alice Kowalski's door. They were still away on vacation. Mrs. Kowalski was recovering from a nasty bullet wound that had come near to breaking her shoulder. A bullet shot by a serial bomber who's real target had been Tony Alfano's head. Four inches, either way, might have resulted in either his or Alice's death. Sometimes it was better to be lucky than good—good and dead.

After setting his shoulder holster and revolver on the counter, he poured two fingers of whiskey and began to slice the potatoes. He browned the ground chuck in an iron fry pan, his primary kitchen appliance, on the small electric burner. In fifteen minutes, he'd made himself a relatively decent hash. He cracked two eggs in the mixture and folded them together. Heinz catsup was the garnish.

A small radio sat on the shelf behind the sink. Alfano turned it on and rotated the dial until he found WMAQ. The sweet sounds of the Earl Hines Orchestra from the Grand Terrace Ballroom on South Parkway filled his small apartment. 'Fatha' Hines was a keyboard playing institution and his orchestra played the type of jazz that Alfano liked. He sat down at his small kitchen table, flipped open his notebook and began to write single-line notes between mouthfuls of hash and sips of whiskey. It was his way of laying out the facts; he couldn't drag the corkboard around, so his notebooks were the second best thing. After dinner, he poured another drink and sloshed it around in the crystal tumbler he'd picked up at a rummage sale at St. Benedict's. He lit a cigarette, thinking that he hated introspection, whether it was about a crime or his own life. It was the facts that counted, not the Freudian bullshit the docs claimed made up the seriously fucked-up criminals he dealt with daily. He no more wanted to crawl into their skin and see the world from their degenerate point of view than to spend time looking at his. It was all a waste of time and brain cells.

They were the bad guys, period. They all needed to be caught and put in jail. Some needed more than catching, they needed punishment; some needed to be dead.

He'd never considered himself a sword of vengeance; that was for others. What he wanted was to solve the crime: collect the clues and piece together the puzzle left by the bad guys. He left psychological mumbo-jumbo and prosecution to the DA and his pack of sympathetic lawyers, who angled anything and everything. And for some in the DA's office, it was how much they could tap the dirt bag for. Money ruled everything, and downtown it was money and power. A lot was changing with the legalization of booze, but Alfano knew that one thing would never change—human nature. Maybe someday the doc's might find a way to make something of the mumbo-jumbo, today he didn't care.

He sipped his Canadian and thought of the last case that all came crashing down on the day of the opening of the Century of Progress World's Fair. The bomber, the rocket ship hung from the cable six hundred feet above the fair traveling from tower to tower, the jump from the open door. He thought of Gini, the look on her face as she'd pressed a revolver against her breast and pulled the trigger. Her expression had been peaceful, a smile, like she was given a present and couldn't wait to open it. *Fuck.*

He poured another two fingers in the glass. It was all fucked, and he'd been caught in the middle. He'd loved her, given his heart another chance, and for that, she'd tried to have him killed. *What the fuck was that?*

He went back to his notepad. There was a spot of water on the page from the single tear he hadn't meant to shed. The ink bled, turning the line he'd just written into a scrawl. It had all happened less than a month ago, but to Tony it felt like it was last year, fucking last century. He could have helped her; it could have worked out. No one would have known; he was the only one who knew. But she'd taken the easy way and blown her broken heart to pieces.

He ripped off the tear-splattered note sheet, wadded it into a ball and pitched it toward the round wastebasket. It hit the rim, bounced up about six inches and disappeared.

TONY dragged himself out of bed and stood looking out the open window. It was still dark; all he saw were rooftops and parts of neon signs. During the night it had cooled some, but not so much that it made sleeping any easier. His shorts were damp with sweat. He stretched and tried to gather what wits he had about him, then pulled on his trousers and slipped his suspenders over his bony shoulders. He looked about the disaster that was the kitchen part of his apartment. Thirty minutes later, the dishes were clean and the empty whiskey bottle and other miscellaneous leavings from dinner were gone to the incinerator and trash. He promised himself a decent shower later at the YMCA; he disliked taking a bath in this weather, and the corroded showerhead in his bathroom barely leaked enough water to mimic a shower.

Ten minutes later he was headed down Ashland Avenue to Racine Street. McDunnah had beaten him to the station by twenty minutes.

"Coffee's made."

"You will be sainted, McDunnah. Sure has hell, sainted."

"Good morning to you, too."

"Sainted, you Irishman, sainted."

Alfano inhaled the steam rising from the cup McDunnah delivered to his desk.

"Muggy again today, Detective," the sergeant said.

"As if anyone needs to be told, I hardly slept."

Alfano sipped the hot coffee; in this heat it seemed almost cool.

"The wife was up most of the night," McDunnah mentioned. "The weather's had a real effect on her."

He told Alfano that there'd already been a call from the police captain up in Whitefish Bay. According to the captain, things were 'up in the air' there.

"Seems he sent out a senior officer and a beat cop to talk with the DeAngelos. That was about five o'clock last night."

The DeAngelos lived on the northwest side of town, the captain had said. For a Sunday evening, it was quiet; a few people in the neighborhood were out walking. The officers knocked on the door, and nothing. They could see lights on inside, so they knocked on the back door. It opened as they knocked.

"They go in?" asked Alfano.

"No, not right away. The house seemed strange to them. They asked one of the neighbors if the DeAngelos were away, and the man said they never left the house except to go to work, church or the market. 'Nice people, real nice' he said. Always there to help. Their English had a hard Italian edge to it, but almost everyone in that neighborhood is only one or two generations from the Old Country."

"And?"

"They eventually went in. Searched the downstairs and then the upstairs, nothing. They found the cellar door and went down. Here's where the captain about choked up on the phone. Seems that they found Mr. and Mrs. DeAngelo tied to chairs in the basement, both dead. Signs of torture and both looked like they'd been strangled—like their daughter. Jesus, Mary and Joseph, Detective, what the hell is going on?"

Alfano followed up Sergeant McDunnah's summary with a call to the captain in Whitefish Bay. The coroner there had confirmed the strangulation and torture. The police had no idea why or by whom. Neighbors had seen the DeAngelos out on their front porch on Saturday evening, about 9:00 o'clock;

everything seemed normal. The neighbors hadn't known about the daughter's death until one of the patrolmen let slip the reason they were there. Accordingly, the whole neighborhood was on edge.

Alfano learned from the captain that Mary Ann DeAngelo's parents had arrived from Italy just after the war. Mr. DeAngelo worked hard and had a small tourist shop in town. His wife taught at the local college and spoke excellent English; she'd been a university professor or something like it in Rome. They'd come to America to escape the fascists. When asked if they were commies, the neighbors didn't know or if they did, wouldn't say. Mary Ann had gone to Chicago because a friend thought he might know of a job. She'd been there about two months, working. The captain did not believe the murders were motivated by a robbery because too many valuables were left lying about.

"Can you tell me this, Sergeant? Who the hell would kill an entire family?" he said to McDunnah, as the two men stood looking at the board.

"On the Saints, I haven't a clue. Vengeance is always a reason, especially among you Italians. *Vendetta*."

Alfano looked at McDunnah and raised an eyebrow.

"You know damn well it's a reason, Detective. It has been and always will be. And from what you've said, they certainly weren't working class. They were educated and fled Mussolini and his thugs. Maybe they left some unresolved issues in Italy."

"Maybe. Look, over the past ten years, you and I have seen my countrymen do some very nasty things to each other, and when we've seen this kind of torture it was for information, not vengeance."

"True, your people are pretty good at information gathering."

"And the Irish?"

"More clinical—bombs and assassinations. We are less,

how you say, brutal."

"Bullshit, and you know it, but I get your meaning," Alfano told him. "According to the sequence, it's my guess the same person murdered Mary Ann and then went to Milwaukee to question her parents. When whoever it is got what they wanted, they killed the parents. Whatever Mary Ann said led the killer to her family. Now all we have to do is find out the who and the why."

6

CARLA ACERBI parked the car, a black Oldsmobile touring sedan, in the basement stall assigned to her unit. She was exhausted. It had been more than forty-eight hours since she'd had any meaningful sleep, and the coffee jag she'd been on since Wisconsin had ebbed and sapped her strength. The drive up and back from Milwaukee had taken almost twenty-four hours. She'd taken a risk and slept for an hour at a highway rest stop outside of Kenosha and eaten breakfast near Zion.

The DeAngelos had been less than helpful. They did confirm that three young men had visited them ten days earlier. Even after she'd offered to spare the wife, the man wouldn't say more than that the men lived in Chicago. No, he didn't know their last names, but they were students at Loyola.

"*Nomi*," she'd demanded in Italian.

"We won't tell you anything, you fascist bitch," Mrs. DeAngelo said.

"We will see. I'm very good at this, as you will see," Acerbi replied.

An hour later she had first names: Lucca, Matteo, and Sal. She'd been kind enough not to tell the couple that their daughter was already dead. In fact, she'd used the girl as one last bit of leverage to convince them to tell her everything. When she was sure she had as much as she could extract, she left them in the basement, mutilated and lifeless. Everything she used, including gloves and bloody over-shirt, she deposited in a garbage bin outside a market in Kenosha.

Since leaving Rome more than a month earlier, Acerbi had been focused on Chicago and the information given by her commanding officer: "Our informer at the Sapienza Rome University says that the communists will do anything to try and embarrass our government and our leader. With the naïve Americans soon to open their World's Fair in Chicago, there is a chance these traitors will use this international stage as a way to embarrass Italy and Il Duce."

Acerbi's assignment was straightforward: find out what the communists intended to do and stop it, using any means possible.

Her commandant in the secret police had pushed an envelope toward her across the mahogany desktop. Acerbi picked it up and removed the two pages, and quickly scanned them. Yes, it was a plot, undefined, but the informant said that information he had gathered from sources at the Sapienza University of Rome was clear. Students, a number unknown, were in Chicago, studying at Loyola University. These communists had decided to take an action against the Italian government and would use their cover as foreign students to dramatically humiliate the fascists. Acerbi finished reading and looked at her commandant.

"This cannot be allowed to happen," he said. "We have the name of a family that has contacts with these conspirators; it was not given up easily."

Per the commandant's instructions, Acerbi had started with the daughter, Mary Ann DeAngelo, known to be living in Chicago.

"Do what is necessary to find these saboteurs; they are traitors to Italy. And do what you must to stop them," he told

Carla.

She had crossed the Atlantic on the *Rex* as a tourist, with papers that stated her name as Donna Delucca, cultural historian and liaison to the Italian mission set up to assist the Italian company building the Italian exhibit at the Century of Progress World's Fair. When she arrived in Chicago on the *Twentieth Century Limited* train, she did not stop to introduce herself at their offices but headed directly to the apartment arranged for her by her government. The automobile came with the apartment. Her second set of papers listed her name as Carla Acerbi, a well-known family name in Italy. Even a great nineteenth-century Italian adventurer carried the name; translated to English it roughly meant 'heartless.' Her commandant had chosen the name and when he told her, she smiled.

"Sir, I will try to live up to my name," she said. "I will not fail you."

"It will not be me you fail. It will be Italy and our leader."

After her arrival and before her abduction of the DeAngelo daughter, Acerbi laid the groundwork for her investigation. She visited the Loyola University campus and met with the woman in charge of admissions, hoping to collect the names of students enrolled from Italy.

"I'm eager to find countrymen who might help us at the fair," she said, offering a plausible reason for her curiosity. "They might be able to help with translations and communication."

The woman had been cooperative, but the list she gave Acerbi was extensive, and many on it would be residents of Chicago's Italian neighborhoods. If she started contacting people on the list, she might scare off the men she was searching for. They would be paranoid and any inquiries would alert them. She'd decided to start with the daughter as a way to get to the one person who might know who the traitors were—the girl's father.

The plan had succeeded to a degree; she checked the three first names against the list. There were more than a dozen matches. She had much more to do.

IN THE heart of the Italian neighborhood on Taylor Street, in a basement apartment, three young men sat at a roughly hewn round table, drinking red wine. The shades were closed, and even though it was the middle of the day, the room was dark. The heat of the previous week had lessened and the cellar was, at least, tolerable although the air stunk of gasoline. The men spoke in hushed voices.

"Signore DeAngelo does not answer our calls. This concerns me," the man called Lucca said.

"It should," Sal Rizzo said. "Since we began this, they have always maintained contact."

The DeAngelos had supplied the men with three flare guns, four sticks of dynamite and a schedule of the events at the fair. Since arriving back in Chicago, the three had been actively collecting five-gallon cans of gasoline that were now stacked against the back wall of the basement apartment. Through family connections in Chicago, they had been able to procure two revolvers, a long barrel .38 and the other a short .38 Detective Special, although they all agreed that they would try to avoid using the pistols.

Looking at the stack of cans, Lucca said, "I feel like I'm living inside an automobile full of gasoline. When it was so hot, I couldn't even sleep in here. Thankfully, the store above is closed. They would be asking about the smell."

"That's why I chose it," Sal said. "My cousin represents a lot of apartment owners. He gave us a deal."

"Some deal. My parents think I'm living in the lap of luxury at that price," Lucca answered.

"You didn't have to tell them."

"It was the cost, not the quality of the accommodations," Lucca said, looking around the basement. A counter with a hot plate stood in for a kitchen, and the couch doubled as his bedroom. At least the bathroom had a door.

Lucca Barone was born in Rome. His family's wealth came from the banking industry. Matteo Cavallo was from Naples, and his parents were university professors. Salvatore Rizzo had grown up in Genoa and was the first in his family of fishermen to go to university. All three men were twenty-one and single, not that they hadn't had opportunities. They'd met at Sapienza Rome University and become fast friends; they also hated the fascists. From this hatred grew a fixation with Italy's version of Marxist communism. Theirs was an infatuation more in its defiance of Mussolini than a particular attraction to Marxism as a political reality. The chance to visit America and attend Loyola University during their third year of studies had come via the recommendation of one of their professors.

"There is much you can learn in America," the professor had told them. "Most especially their political decadence and treatment of the workers. But I talk too much; you will see."

"When were you in America, *professore*?" Matteo had asked. "It might be different."

"Oh, I have never been there. It is too decadent. But be assured, it is as I have said."

Three weeks after they were offered the opportunity and its generous stipend, the professor met with them at a small café near the university. Across the street, the massive Verano Cemetery stretched into the hills.

"My boys, there is something else that you have to do when you are in Chicago."

The professor put a finger to his lips and looked about the café. It was relatively empty this time of day, and he gave a satisfied nod.

"It is important to our cause and the country," he said.

"I knew it," Matteo said. "You never get something for nothing. You want us to smuggle something in or out. We had many great smugglers in my family, so why the hell not!"

"We do not need you to smuggle anything into America. In a manner of speaking, we want to stop someone from leaving."

The three friends exchanged puzzled looks.

"Yes, I can tell from the donkey looks, you are confused," said their teacher. "All I am asking is for you to perform an action against the government of Mussolini that will put a thorn in his shoe and humiliate him in the eyes of the Americans."

"How?" Lucca wanted to know. "There is nothing in America and most especially Chicago that could be connected to Il Duce. Especially something we three students could do."

"Ah, you are so young and naïve, but that is why I like you. Don't you read the popular magazines? Chicago is going to open a colossal World's Fair next May, and the Americans have been courting Italy for three years to open an exhibition celebrating the fascists' glorious accomplishments. From what I've seen of the drawings, they may succeed. I have a cousin in Chicago who is working on the building and even he says it is quite spectacular."

"Okay, so you want us to send you photos?" Lucca said, a smirk on his face.

"And you call yourselves revolutionaries," the professor said darkly. "No, we need to make a statement against this regime, and what better place than where his ego would be most on display."

"So you want us to blow up the building," Sal said, with a laugh. "No problem, all we would need is a hundred kilos of dynamite and luck. But I assure you *professore*, this boy from Genoa isn't going to commit suicide so that someone can embarrass an asshole."

"No, no, nothing so mundane and besides, people would get hurt. We have in mind something even more spectacular."

The three looked at their professor. He was clearly not joking, which had them fully baffled.

"More spectacular? What?" Matteo asked.

"We have found out that sometime in late June, General Italo Balbo, Il Duce's second-in-command, will fly his fleet of seaplanes to Chicago to help celebrate the opening of the fair. I imagine it will be something to see."

"So, you want us to take photos of the planes and send them to you?" Sal said, only half joking.

"No, my boys. We want you to blow them up."

7

CAPTAIN WOLFOWITZ, the chief of police of Whitefish Bay, told Tony via telephone the next morning that the DeAngelos, whose bodies had been found late the previous afternoon, had both been dead at least twenty-four hours, possibly longer. Wolfowitz had called in forensic help from Milwaukee. This had been the most brutal murder, actually murders, that the small town of Whitefish Bay had ever seen. When Alfano mentioned coming up to see the scene and the bodies, Wolfowitz had no objection.

"If it hadn't been for your sergeant there, not sure if we would have found them for a long while," Wolfowitz said. "According to neighbors, the DeAngelos had been planning on a vacation now that school was over. They wouldn't have been missed for weeks."

"Did they have other children?" Alfano asked, picking up on the captain's comment about school being out of session.

"Only the daughter in Chicago. It's a damn shame about her, and now the two of them dead. The neighbors said they were both real smart—book smart but down-to-earth, good people. Everyone seems shocked by what happened."

"My guess is they were more than what they seemed."

Later that morning, Alfano left the station and drove

north on State Highway 32 toward Wisconsin. Along the open stretches between towns, the road was nothing more than gravel treated with tar to keep the dust down. There was a weak breeze off Lake Michigan that, along with opening the windows of the Packard, gave Alfano slight relief from the heat and humidity. Whitefish Bay was a lakefront village of one-story brick and clapboard-sided homes. Alfano drove straight to the police station, shook hands with Wolfowitz, and the pair continued on to the crime scene in the captain's vehicle. The DeAngelo house was on the north side of town, just eight blocks from the police station. En route, Alfano caught glimpses of Lake Michigan between the houses fronting the lake.

"Nice neighborhood," he offered.

"Yeah, quiet. Most people work in Milwaukee and the north side. We've got a mix of a lot of nationalities: Poles, like yours truly, Swedes, Germans, and even a few Italians."

A small cluster of local residents huddled across the street from the DeAngelo home, where a police car sat out front. A uniformed officer was stationed at the front door of the house. The patrolman saluted as Alfano followed the chief inside.

"The house was undisturbed, leastwise as we could see," Wolfowitz told Tony. "It was just as you see it, neat and very clean. But not like it had been cleaned up afterward; Mrs. DeAngelo kept a clean house, as my wife would say."

Alfano walked through the rooms; nothing stood out or seemed out of place. In fact, in some ways, it reminded him of his mother's home of twenty years earlier, with Italian ceramics and plates, glassware in a cabinet, crocheted doilies and armchair covers. In the center of the large dining table sat a vase filled with roses, presumably plucked from the manicured rose bushes that lined the walk to the front door. The flowers were still somewhat fresh; maybe a dozen fallen petals lay on the polished surface of the table.

"The bodies were found in the basement?" Alfano asked.

"This way."

At the back of the kitchen, a door opened to a steep stairway that disappeared into a dark basement. Wolfowitz clicked on the light, which did little more than light the stairs.

"Was the light on when your man showed up?"

"No, he distinctly remembers that it was not on—he had to fumble around, trying to find the switch there."

"Did you check for fingerprints on the switch or the railing?"

"There was this smudge of blood near the switch. It's here."

Wolfowitz pointed to a dark stain below the round light switch with its black toggle screwed to the wood paneling that lined the stairway.

"But nothing on the steps. My guy didn't see the smudge when he entered. Some spots that may be blood are on the steps. The guys from Milwaukee are figuring it out."

They stopped when they reached the bare concrete floor of the basement; the underground room felt twenty degrees cooler than the upstairs.

"I would have spent the last few days down here after this past week of heat," Wolfowitz said. "It's almost pleasant."

"Almost," Alfano said, as he played his flashlight around the room.

Wooden shelves lined the walls and were stacked with glass jars full of fruits and pickles. The lower shelves held boxes with labels, all in Italian. An American flag on a stand leaned against the far corner next to another furled flag; Alfano recognized the colors as possibly Italian. In the center of the room were two stout oaken chairs, positioned so that they faced each other. Strips of rope hung from the chair arms and more were scattered on the floor.

"Lights?" Wolfowitz asked.

"Yeah," Alfano answered.

He heard the tinkle of a thin chain hitting ceramic and glass. After multiple clicks of switches, the room was bathed in the light from three overhead bare light bulbs; long chains hung to shoulder height from each socket mounted to the ceiling. With the lights on, dried pools of a black substance were visible beneath the chairs.

"You said they were strangled?" Alfano said, looking at the blood.

"They each still had a length of rope around their necks, a loop and pull setup."

Alfano nodded. The killer would have been able to apply increasing pressure until the victim passed out.

"The blood was from their severely damaged hands—fingers broken, crushed in fact," Wolfowitz said. "Their feet and arms were bound to the chairs."

"Was Mr. DeAngelo a big man?"

"Yes, maybe one hundred eighty pounds, just under six feet."

"How would he have let this happen without a fight?"

"We think that he was not home when this started. Neighbors say he was at his store. He did a lot of his inventory and preparation for the week, and with the heat, there was a big demand for his ice cream. He usually got home around six p.m. But no one we talked to saw what time he arrived home on Sunday."

"So whoever killed them may have arrived early and tied up Mrs. DeAngelo, questioned her, then waited for the husband. With threats to the wife, he would have been more manageable."

"Right. Then they could have done anything."

"They?" Alfano asked. "You think there was more than one person?"

"You think one person could do all this?"

"Look at the floor."

Alfano used his flashlight to point to spots, smudges, and a partial footprint on the concrete.

"Whoever it was left tracks, and they all seem to be from the same shoes. Actually, it looks like they were wrapped with socks or something. Some of the prints have fabric patterns; yes, I would say socks over the shoes."

Wolfowitz studied the footprints.

"Damn. We missed the sock covering. The floor had dried by the time we arrived."

"This footprint here seems to be the most complete," Alfano said, pointing his light. "Do you notice something else?"

Wolfowitz studied the smudge and cloth pattern, then stepped next to it and placed his right foot near the smudge.

"Damn, a woman's print, or I'd guess a very small man."

"My guess too, a woman. Your shoe is what, an eleven?"

"Yes."

"That print can't be more than a woman's size seven, narrow. My guess is that when she came to the door she didn't seem like a threat to Mrs. DeAngelo, who let her in, and once she was in—"

"All she had to do was tie up the wife and then wait," Wolfowitz said.

Alfano nodded.

"Were they gagged?" he asked the captain.

"Yes, with strips of towel. They matched some we found in a box on the shelf there."

"The ropes?"

"None we found here. We believe the killer brought the ropes with her."

"The damage was done with what?"

"Pliers, nails, and a hammer. There was a box of tools on the floor. They are in evidence bags at the station."

"So she wasn't completely prepared, but then again most

people have these things lying about. Knives, hammers, ice picks—the usual stuff," Alfano said.

He walked around the basement and studied the jars and boxes. After several minutes, he turned to Wolfowitz.

"The boxes are full of notes on various projects they must have been interested in. It says here in Italian, 'Fascists in Rome.' The other labels refer to Italian cities and political groups. This one says 'University of Rome'; I would guess they thought being five thousand miles away left them safe from whoever they were hiding from in Italy."

"That could make some sense, Detective. It's pretty easy to hide in plain sight around here—most people leave each other alone."

After they had left the house, Alfano and Wolfowitz spent an hour in the morgue, talking with the county coroner. As he looked at the bodies, Alfano couldn't help but notice that the damage to the hands of the DeAngelos was similar to the crushed fingers of their daughter. He grew more certain that whoever had done this was the same person, and shockingly a woman.

"This is the work of a professional killer," he said to Wolfowitz. "Their daughter was dumped in the rain after she was killed so that any evidence on the body would be lost. We still don't know where Mary Ann was killed. At least we know that much with the parents."

He turned to the coroner.

"Anything else?"

"These," the man said.

The folded cloth he held up looked familiar to Alfano. The fabric had been stuffed into their mouths.

"Then the gags were applied, or most likely reapplied, afterward," the coroner said.

"Have you unrolled the scarves?" Tony asked.

"Yes."

The coroner unfurled one of the thin strips of fabric.

"It's the fascist flag of Italy," Alfano told the other men, as they studied the design. "A flag like this was also found in the daughter."

"In?"

The coroner shook his head when Alfano explained.

Wolfowitz said, "Son of a bitch. Why kill an entire family? I've been racking my brain since your sergeant called; who could do this and why?"

"My sergeant, a generous, big-hearted mick, says it's because we Italians will carry a vendetta for years. However, these poor souls were tortured for information, slowly and methodically. They were probably asked questions until they gave the right answers; then they were killed. The daughter was killed on Friday night, the mother and father two days later. Someone is collecting information about something or someone, and it's my guess that information may lead to another killing, and soon. Not here, but back in Chicago."

"Can't say I'm not happy to hear that. I'm not sure this small town could handle another murder like this."

"And you think my town can?"

"Detective Alfano, I wouldn't wish this on anyone, but Chicago has millions of people. My town barely has ten thousand. You have resources; I have six deputies, and two are part-time. So yeah, I think your town can handle it. Sorry, but that's why a lot of people live here. Because things like this don't happen here."

"Yeah, I get it, Captain, but this crime *did* happen here and your sweet little lakefront town isn't a virgin anymore. Welcome to the big leagues."

8

ALFANO filled more space on the corkboard with copies of the crime scene photos he'd received from Wolfowitz. The captain had promised to pass along the coroner's report as soon as it was completed.

"Goddamn brutal, Detective," McDunnah said, as he looked over the photos of the DeAngelos tied to chairs. "Whoever did this has to have a stone cold heart."

"Crazies, Sergeant, crazies. There is something not wired right in their brain. And we know, if there's one wrong wire there are others, frayed and ready to short out. They will be unpredictable, one killing after another. But I think there's something else going on here."

"The torturing for information?" McDunnah offered.

"Yeah, pretty high stakes, I think. That couple had gone through a lot before they told their killer anything."

"You sure they told her what she wanted to know? You say you're sure she's a woman?"

"Yes to both, or at least what the killer expected to hear. I think she would have torn the place apart if not. Yet, they found it neat and in order. So, yeah, I think she got what she wanted."

"Now all we have to do is figure out what the hell that is."

"Yeah, there's that too."

"While you were heading back, Chief Wolfowitz called."

McDunnah opened a folded piece of paper. Handwritten notes covered one side.

"He said that one of the neighbors thought they might have seen the car the killer used. He would've come forward sooner but left on Sunday afternoon for a fishing trip. When he got back, he of course heard the news from the neighbors. Says he saw a new black Oldsmobile touring sedan parked a few blocks away the afternoon he headed out of town. New but with a skirt of mud around its running boards, which made him think the driver came up after the rain."

"Up? How did this guy know it wasn't one of the neighbors?"

"The captain asked that. The witness said that with the economy the way it is, there's not many new cars out there. He also knows everyone in the neighborhood, plus he saw that the plates were muddy and from Illinois."

"Not a chance at a plate number, I guess?"

"None. Never thought about it, he said. It was a nice car, the windows were down, probably due to the heat, he remembered noticing that. When the police asked around about the car, no one else remembered seeing it. But then again, no one had visitors from Illinois that day either."

"So we aren't completely sure it was the killer's car," Alfano said.

"No, but it's a good bet. And right now, I'd take one serious clue to stick on that board."

McDunnah went to his desk and returned with a single sheet of paper.

"I remember seeing this," he said, and showed Alfano an advertisement for an Oldsmobile, torn from a recent issue of *Look* magazine. The sergeant put two thumbtacks through the corners of the photo page and added it to the board.

"Is it possible to track down this car?" Alfano asked him. "Black Oldsmobile, 1932 or '33?"

"The fellow was adamant that it was a '33—the softer lines and the raked-back grill. I know what he meant; it's pretty easy to tell last year's model from this year. I'll see what pops up," McDunnah promised. "There couldn't be more than a few hundred in the city."

Alfano poured himself another cup of coffee and scrawled a few lines about the car in his notebook. He'd updated his notes the night before, when he stopped at a motor court to get a few hours sleep. He looked at the clock on the wall—10:00 a.m.—rubbed the back of his neck before turning back to the board, looking over the photos and the notes, occasionally referring to his notebook. The whole thing was a disconnected mess. Other than his gut, he had little to go on.

The squad room phone rang. A few minutes later, McDunnah handed him another note.

"We got lucky. One of the roommates found a paper with the address of where Mary Ann DeAngelo worked. It's on Wacker near Wabash, the new skyscraper called the Jewelers Building. They found it after you left on Sunday."

Mary Ann had worked in the secretarial pool for a small insurance company that was headquartered in Kansas City. No, the roommate hadn't talked to anyone at Mary Ann's place of work, McDunnah said, when Tony asked.

"She said she couldn't bring herself to that," the sergeant told him. "We don't know what the people Miss DeAngelo worked with know or have heard."

McDunnah had, however, learned the name of the local office's business manager. It was a Mr. Jamison.

IT TOOK ten minutes to get to the Jewelers Building. When he parked out front, Alfano looked up the stone façade of the forty-story building and marveled at the detail and height. It dwarfed everything on Wacker Drive, and the views north to the Chicago River weren't too bad either. When it had opened four or five years back, it was one of the tallest buildings west of New York City. He put a card that read 'Police Business' on the dash and left the Packard at the curb. Inside, the lobby was impressively adorned with marble and gilded trim. Tony imagined the gilded elevators were like the ones that took you to heaven. A guard sat behind a marble counter. Alfano flipped his badge and the man straightened in his chair.

"Don't I know you?" he said, squinting up at the detective.

The guard slid his eyeglasses down his nose.

"Yeah, Detective Alfano at Racine. I'd have thought you retired or were dead after all the shit from the last ten years. O'Rourke, Finnian, sir. The fellows called me Finn."

Alfano looked back at him.

"Sure, Finn, I remember. Didn't you take a bullet from one of the North Siders when we hit one of their breweries?"

"Damn near broke my leg in two. Big fucking caliber pistol. Couldn't do the job anymore so I retired. Not much money, but this is a good gig for a gimpy Irishman. What can I help you with, Detective?"

"I'm here to see a fellow with Prairie River Insurance, name of Jamison. You know him?"

"Indeed I do. He's a snappy dresser, sharp nose and face, thinks he's a ladies' man. Some late nights he waltzes through here with a good-looking gal on his arm. I understand he lives in Kansas City, and I heard some of the girls in his office say he's married. None of my business; I just make sure that the riffraff doesn't get past this desk. Tough times."

"So I've been told. Do you know if he's in?"

"No, sir. I just came on at ten o'clock. If he's in town, he would have already been in at eight. He's punctual."

"Lives in Kansas City?"

"Yes, sir. Comes into town once a month for a week, then

home. From the way he acts, no one would guess he's married."

"Floor?"

"The company is on fourteen, has most of the floor. The elevator opens right onto their lobby. There's always a good-looking gal at the reception desk. Just tell Davey. He'll make sure you get there."

"Thanks, Finn. By the way, I'd appreciate it if you didn't call to let them know I'm coming. This is an official visit."

"Wouldn't think of it."

Alfano walked to the elevators. The open car held one man, an older Negro gentleman with short gray hair. His brass pocket nameplate said 'David.' He sat on a stool in front of a bank of buttons.

"You Davey?"

"Yes, sir, saw you talking with Finn. You a police officer?"

"That obvious?"

"No, Finn isn't usually that polite. Where to?"

"Fourteen, Prairie River Insurance."

"Fourteen it is, sir."

As the elevator car rose, Davey hummed a few lines from a sweet piece by Louis Armstrong.

"That's *Dinah*, isn't it?"

"You know your tunes, officer. Yeah, the dude is from my hometown, New Orleans. I catch him when he's in town, out at the Regal and Lincoln Gardens."

"I saw him at the Regal maybe two years ago," replied Alfano. "Hot night, hot band."

The elevator slowed to a stop. Davey pulled the interior metal grill doors apart and then opened the outside elevator doors.

"From what I see, you are not here to buy insurance," Davey remarked.

"No sir, I am not."

9

ALFANO walked directly to the receptionist's desk. He heard Davey humming as the attendant closed the elevator doors. The young woman at the desk, blond, oval-faced, wearing a gray business suit with a broad, white shirt collar, looked up from her typewriter. She flashed her baby blues at Alfano.

"May I be of help, sir?" she said softly.

The nameplate on her desk read 'Nancy Noonan.'

Alfano showed her his gold star.

"Mr. Jamison, please."

"Is Mr. Jamison expecting you, officer? I don't have you on his calendar."

She smiled warmly.

"Of course, you don't. He didn't know I would be coming. So please go through those doors and tell him that Detective Anthony Alfano is here for an important meeting, one he'd better take."

Alfano's stern demeanor cut through the pleasantness. Nancy Noonan's eyes grew larger, then narrowed to a displeased glare.

"I will ask if Mr. Jamison is taking visitors."

She rose, spun on her dark gray pumps and stepped through the door directly behind her desk. It closed with a click.

Alfano toured the reception area; overstuffed leather furniture populated the room. The floor was a checkered black-and-white marble; the walls were decorated with large photos of farms, grain silos, and bridges, also black and white. Stacks of business magazines covered the low end tables. On the far wall hung a large framed colored poster of the Century of Progress World's Fair; three golden spires dominated the image. He turned at the sound of Miss Noonan's heels on the far side of the door. She opened and held the door for an angular gentleman, tall, thin-faced, slight fashionable mustache, gray on his temples under a full head of dark hair. He wore a very expensive beige linen suit. He walked to Alfano and put his hand out. His handshake was firm.

"Detective Alfano, sorry to have taken so much time to receive you. I was on the phone to New York and didn't want to lose the connection. Please follow me. Do you care for coffee?"

"Yes, thanks," Alfano answered, keeping his expression neutral as he looked at the strip of bandage that crossed Mr. Jamison's face from cheek to cheek, passing directly over his nose. Both eyes were black and blue.

"Miss Noonan, coffee, please," said Jamison, then turned and proceeded through the door, with Alfano in his wake. They finally ended up in a corner office, overlooking the Chicago River.

"Nice view," Alfano said, admiring the river and the lumber barge that slowly worked its way against the current, upriver from Lake Michigan.

"What can I help you with, Detective?"

"Does a Miss Mary Ann DeAngelo work here?"

"She does, but we have not seen her since last Friday," Jamison answered, after a moment's pause. "She has left no messages or called and, frankly, we are concerned. I give fair latitude to my employees but if she doesn't come in tomorrow, she's through. I have a dozen girls waiting for her spot."

"Nice attitude, Jamison. She won't be coming in tomorrow or ever, she's dead. Her body was found Saturday morning. According to a few people, you were the last person to be with her the previous night. I was told by reputable sources that the two of you were on a date. Tsk, tsk, Mr. Jamison, you being a married man."

The news clearly rocked Jamison. Alfano watched his body language go from in control to nervous distraction, to obvious concern.

"How?" Jamison asked, trying to light a cigarette with his very shaky right hand.

Miss Noonan had entered the office in time to overhear enough that she let out a small cry, just managing not to drop the coffee tray she carried. Jamison took a sharp look at her.

"You may go, Miss Noonan, and not a word to anyone on the floor."

He turned quickly to Alfano.

"Is that a proper request?"

"Yes, thank you. I will have questions, if you don't mind, for some of your employees. But for the moment, I need to ask you a few."

The door clicked shut as Miss Noonan left. Alfano was absolutely positive that in minutes the floor would be alive with the news. In ten minutes everyone would have an alibi, assuming they needed one. He was also sure that more than a couple of Jamison's employees would love to spill the beans on their boss, who had filled two cups with coffee and was about to hand one to Alfano.

"Thanks, I've had more than enough," Alfano said.

Jamison looked bewildered; he set down one of the cups and motioned toward the two leather chairs in the corner of the office.

"Yes, I was out having dinner with Mary Ann," he said,

when they were seated. "She's a delightful girl—I mean, she was. We had dinner at the Cape Cod room with some friends then went to a small jazz club where I'm a member. There was a disagreement with one of the patrons, and I understand that Miss DeAngelo left with that patron. I did not see them leave."

"That when you had your nose busted?"

"Yes, there was a misunderstanding and before I could defend myself, I was attacked, kicked, and my nose broken. This is the first day since Saturday that I have been able to chew anything."

Ignoring Jamison's obvious plea for sympathy, Alfano asked, "The name of the club?"

"I don't wish to get them in trouble."

"Without an acceptable alibi, I suggest that you're the man in trouble. The club's name, Mr. Jamison."

Jamison looked thoughtful, sipped his coffee before answering.

"It's on the near West Side, the Lychee Club. It's run by a woman named Mai Lee. I frequent it when I'm in town. The music is always top-notch, and she's a good friend."

"And I've heard the smoke's not bad either. I wouldn't take you for an opium fiend."

"Opium? Never. And I wouldn't know. I go there for the music and the bar. A very good bar."

"Mr. Jamison," Alfano said condescendingly, "and you the manager of a large insurance company, I would have thought nothing escaped you. I also understand the club is very discreet and has excellent political support regarding its entertainment license, considering that it is also a brothel and illegal speakeasy. But you wouldn't know anything about that, being from Kansas City and all."

Small beads of sweat had formed on Jamison's forehead. He dabbed at them with a cloth napkin he took from the tray.

"May I?"

He held up a cigarette.

"You already have one going," Alfano said and pointed to Jamison's desk. "But it is your office, Mr. Jamison. So what really happened that night? In less than an hour, I will have the whole story from Miss Lee—she and I go back a few years. I have never seen anyone more interested in protecting her own very scrawny butt than Miss Lee. She would throw anyone under a bus to protect herself. That's a good friend to have."

Jamison left the cigarette to burn in the ashtray on his desk and lit a fresh one. He'd been out with Miss DeAngelo merely to assess her professional credits and experience, Jamison said. While he was showing her around the establishment, she accidentally slipped and screamed from the pain of a twisted ankle. As he attempted to massage the girl's tortured foot, a woman had busted through the door, knocked him to the floor and kicked him in the face.

Alfano looked up from his notebook.

"A woman?"

"Yes, she was in the parlor when we arrived. Now, *she's* the one who was smoking opium. Miss DeAngelo talked with her for a few minutes while I discussed some issues with Miss Lee. They seemed to have hit it off."

"Had you seen her before? What did this woman look like?"

"No, I'd never seen her at the club, but then again a lot of people visit Miss Lee's club. I only visit when I'm in town. The woman? She was one of your people."

"Say again."

"Italian, but her accent said recent to this country."

Jamison inhaled deeply from his cigarette, closed his eyes.

"Tall, striking, she was dressed in a classy striped suit, and had dark eyes—very athletic looking," he told Alfano. "Detective, I've never been to Italy, but between Miss DeAngelo and whoever this broad was, you have some very nice-looking women there."

Alfano just stared at Jamison.

"You're telling me that you, a big man, got your nuts handed to you by a woman? Son of a bitch, she the one who busted your nose?"

"I slipped."

"Like Miss DeAngelo slipped? I get it. Let me put this another way; you were there to seduce Miss DeAngelo, or whatever you call your brand of romance, have your fun then return her to the secretarial pool. Nice guy. Unfortunately for you, in sweeps this warrior Valkyrie, busts you up, then takes the girl away. That what really happen?"

Jamison looked out the window, then back at the detective.

"I'm not proud of what I did, but what you said is close enough. However, I didn't see her after that—either of them. I took a cab directly to the hospital. They patched me up, I went home, got drunk and woke up Saturday afternoon. No one saw me after I left the hospital—it was Cook County General. They have the records."

"Be assured I'll check this all out. In fact, it will be fun talking with Miss Lee. I'm sure she will have a lot to add."

Alfano stood and moved to the door.

"Hang around for a few days, Mr. Jamison. I may have a few more questions. I'm sure your family in Kansas City won't mind. By the way, Miss DeAngelo was murdered. Tortured, violated, then strangled. Do you think this woman was capable of doing all that?"

Jamison went pale, lurched out of his chair and sprinted for the small door in the opposite corner of his office. Alfano left to the sounds of Jamison retching into the toilet of his private bathroom.

"I will take that as a yes," the detective said softly.

Out in the reception area, Miss Noonan sat anxiously at her desk. A handkerchief lay on the keyboard of her typewriter. It was obvious she'd been crying. She looked up at the detective.

"Is it true? Was she killed?" she asked, reaching for the handkerchief.

"Yes. Did you know her?"

"Some. She was new to Chicago. We went out a few times for drinks, but she was always quiet. I thought her simple, maybe a little overly protected, even naïve. She was Italian, born in Rome. Very proud of the fact. Her folks live up in Milwaukee—do they know? I have their address here in my book."

"Yes, her parents know," Alfano said.

Sometimes it was better not to tell everything.

"And Mr. Jamison?"—Alfano nodded toward the doorway—"What's his story?"

"I like my job, sir. In fact, I need this job. My mom's been sick and dad, well, we haven't seen him in a few years."

"Understood. Just tell me, did you ever go on a date with Jamison?"

"He asked, but no. I have a steady guy. He works at the *Tribune* as a printer. We're doing okay."

She hesitated, and Alfano gave her an encouraging look.

"Well, if my boyfriend were to hear the stories about Mr. Jamison that are going around, he'd have me leave here this minute. Then he'd probably beat the living shit—sorry, didn't mean to say that, sir."

"That's okay. By any chance, over the last few weeks, did an Italian looking woman drop by looking for a job or for someone? She would be a tall, attractive type, maybe an accent, probably well dressed. She might have stopped for a little information or an interview? Probably had a few questions."

Noonan thought and then said, "Yes, maybe a week ago."

She looked at the calendar on her desk.

"Yes, Monday last week. She was asking about a job and wanted to fill out an application. I told her we weren't hiring, but I would get her the form to fill out. I left to go to person-nel, and when I returned she was gone."

"She didn't leave a name?"

"No, it never got that far. Sorry, is this important?"

"Could be. Anything amiss?"

"Sorry again. Amiss?"

"When you returned, did she forget something, leave something—you know, anything?"

Miss Noonan thought for a moment.

"Well, it's not important, I'm sure, but this drawer was open about an inch. I quickly checked to see if my purse had been stolen, but it was still there, so I figured I'd forgotten to close it."

"What else do you keep there?"

"Just the usual, pens, ink bottle, ribbons for the typewriter, some candies, and my address book."

"May I see your book?"

Miss Noonan retrieved the book and offered it to Alfano. He quickly glanced through it.

"You said you had the address for Mary Ann's parents in here."

"Yes, DeAngelo, she gave it to me as next of kin. I have all the employees' parents or spouses names and addresses here. It's helpful on Mondays, if you know what I mean."

"I do, but it seems there's something missing."

"What?"

"The page with the DeAngelo's Whitefish Bay address."

10

"PRODUCTIVE MORNING?" McDunnah asked, as Alfano walked into the Racine Station. "You look almost chipper."

"I feel chipper. Let's talk."

The sergeant followed Alfano to his desk, and Tony relayed his conversations with Jamison and Miss Noonan. McDunnah attached a large card to the board. A crude drawing of a human face covered the upper two-thirds; the rest of the card was filled with liner notes pertaining to the physical appearance of their quarry.

"You think we are dealing with a woman," McDunnah said. "One who tortures, does unspeakable things, and then kills her victims?"

"Too much coincidence. Did you get a chance to follow up with Mai Lee?"

"Yes, sir. Much of what Jamison told you coincides with her version, but I absolutely believe he was there to take advantage of Miss DeAngelo. Mai Lee says he's a piece of shit but worth a few hundred bucks every few weeks. In her line of work, she puts up with a lot. She said, quote: 'that rousy son a bitch never come back to my prace, I don't fuck'en care. I fro his ass in street'—otherwise I think what Jamison told you was true. Mai Lee didn't know the other woman. It was the first time she'd been to the place. Said a couple of her girls caught on right away about the woman who roughed up Jamison."

"What do you mean, caught on?"

"Well, two of the girls there play on both sides of the tracks, if you know what I mean," McDunnah said uncomfortably. "Me? I don't understand it, but then again I'm Irish and a good Catholic."

"A new twist to put on the picture," Alfano said thoughtfully. "There was a lot of talk about so-called lesbians ten years ago, all modern and such. We busted a few clubs back then. A few of the guys had no clue what to do with a bar full of women. The clubs are less obvious these days, but a few years back I worked with an expert from Northwestern who tried to explain the whole Freudian aspect."

"Freud? Now where do we go from here? You think this was some type of love triangle gone bad, real bad?"

"More than real bad. No, there's more to this, especially with the killings in Wisconsin. There's a lot more."

Alfano pulled out his notebook and began to rewrite his notes from the morning. Nothing he saw even came close to a motive, and he was one detective who believed in motives. There were reasons, even if deranged, for someone's murderous actions. Love, hate, a jilted lover, revenge, an insult, greed, power, or even pathological, there were a thousand reasons. All good in the head of the killer, all bad for his, or in this case her, victim or victims.

Alfano looked up and watched McDunnah rehang the conical receiver of his phone. When he turned toward Tony, the look on the sergeant's face said not good.

"We have another one, this time on the near North Side, in the 28th District, but it sounds familiar. You want to make the call? The captain's name is O'Malley."

"I know him. He's an okay guy. Tell the chief where I'll be;

should be no blowback."

The new police captain for the Racine Station had just transferred in, replacing the previous captain, who had been found dead on the Wabash Street Bridge not more than three weeks earlier. The captain had been murdered by the same bomber who'd tried to bring down the *Tribune* tower. A few days later, the same bomber had tried to blow up the site of the World's Fair. Alfano had solved both crimes on the same day his girlfriend had blown her heart apart.

After stopping at the 28th District Station, Alfano was directed to an address a block off Division Street. Three patrol cars sat out front. The coroner's meat wagon was also parked at the curb, it's double rear doors open expectantly. Captain O'Malley stood on the short walkway, talking to the coroner.

"I will be a son of a bitch. Is that you, Alfano?"

O'Malley stuck his hand out.

The two men shook hands, and Alfano said, "Good to see you, Captain, and you too Coroner Abrahamson."

Alfano turned to O'Malley.

"Italian, tied to a chair, fingers broken, strangled?"

O'Malley shot Alfano a *what the hell?* look.

"Fourth this week," Alfano said.

"Fourth? Tell me."

Alfano lit a cigarette.

"The first was found in a construction site here in Chicago, the second and third, the parents of the first victim, were found in their home outside Milwaukee, and now this one."

He turned to the coroner.

"How long?"

"Body temp and rigor says less than twenty-four hours. It's real bad, Detective, real bad. The poor kid was put through a lot before the guy strangled him."

"My evidence says it's a woman."

"No shit, really?" O'Malley said.

Alfano told them about his week since finding Miss DeAngelo in the rain-filled hole. Both hardened men could only shake their heads.

"Good God," O'Malley said. "Alfano, how the hell could somebody be so cruel? This really sets a new low, and you think a woman?"

"Points that way," Alfano said. "Is the body still there? Can I take a look?"

"Yes, we are waiting for the photographer to finish," O'Malley said, and added, "My guy is taking some notes and filling evidence bags. You beat my detectives; they were at a bar shooting."

"Early in the day for that," Alfano said.

"With the end of Prohibition coming, my guess is that it will never be too early."

They went up the six steps to the porch of the small bungalow that mirrored a hundred others in this part of town. A patrolman stood just outside the wood door. The small vestibule past the doorway barely held the three men; the coroner led the way. Alfano looked into the living room and saw a middle-aged, heavyset woman sitting on the couch. Another woman about the same age sat next to her, holding her hand. The first woman could have passed for his own mother's sister, he thought.

"The kid's mother," O'Malley said. "She's the one who found him. The other is a neighbor."

"Son of a bitch," Alfano said. "A kid?"

"Yes, fellow about twenty. We will get more when we can talk with his mother. She was hysterical when we got here; it's taken more than an hour to calm her down. When my men arrived, they had to bodily carry her up the stairs. Luckily, one of the men speaks Italian, or they would not have gotten her this far."

"Stairs?"

"He's in the basement. It's through the kitchen."

Alfano thought he was reliving Whitefish Bay; the smells in the house were of Italian cooking, the kitchen counters were covered with pans and bowls, garlands of garlic cloves and peppers hung by the window. In one corner of the kitchen, a door stood open. Flashes of light exploded up from the basement.

"Bob, we are coming down."

"Okay, Captain. I'm done."

The voice filled the narrow stairway.

"I'll stay up here," the coroner told the captain. "Not much room down there. I'll be down after you come up."

Alfano followed O'Malley down the stairs. As with the upstairs, the basement reminded him of the DeAngelo basement, but this time, in the middle of the room under a single overhead light bulb was a man in a chair, his head drooping on his chest. Alfano walked slowly around the victim, noticing the hands and feet tied to the heavy chair, and the upper body tied with quarter-inch-thick ropes that wrapped around the chair's back. The dead man was dressed in black slacks and a blood-splattered undershirt. On a small shelf next to the body were common household tools: a ball-peen hammer, pliers, and ice pick. Even in the dim light, it was evident that all the tools were black with blood.

Alfano looked at the fingers of both hands; he wasn't surprised that they were a ghastly mess, twisted, broken, and bloody. He bent down and studied the man's face. A gag filled his open mouth, and a length of rope still hung around his neck. Directly under the light, Alfano could see deep bruising, where the rope had cut into the man's neck.

"Like this in Wisconsin?" O'Malley asked.

"I didn't see the body, only photographs. Nonetheless, much of this scene is very similar, even down to the tools. The killer is opportunistic, using what she can find, household tools and such that most people have. But I don't see any other rope here. My guess is she brought it with her."

"How could a woman take down a kid this size? He's got to be at least one hundred and fifty pounds, and looks fit."

"I'm more interested in why the mother didn't hear all this going on."

The captain replied, "When we finally did get a few questions in, she said she had been at her brother's, on the South Side, for the last few days. Matteo, her son, lived with her. But he had school, so he stayed. She returned this morning on the 'L' to find this."

"Where did he go to school?" Alfano asked, as he continued his assessment of the bloody scene."

"Loyola, international politics. My guy finally got a little of her history out of her."

O'Malley consulted his notes.

"Let's see, they came over from Sicily eighteen years ago, before the war. Last name Bova. Her husband was murdered when the boy was about five, and she came here to live with her brother."

"The one who lives on the South Side?"

"The same. This was when the neighbor arrived, seeing all the commotion and our prowlers. The neighbor said that Mrs. Bova had been remarried about six years ago, but the man was killed when a bar he was working in blew up. She spat out the Irish name O'Banion. Seems he was killed in the nasty follow-up to the Dean O'Banion assassination."

"I was there when they found O'Banion. Very bloody and very bad," Alfano said.

"And all hell broke out for years. Do you think this business now has something to do with O'Banion?"

"No, something else is going on. The killer, if it is the same woman, would have had time to get Bova drunk or slip him a mickey. It still doesn't make sense the only thing in common is that they were Italian and all were immigrants during the last fifteen years."

"That could include half the population of the city. Between us micks and you dagos, shit, there wouldn't be a cab driver in the whole town."

Alfano half smiled. O'Malley's words were at least partly true.

"You got a flashlight?" Alfano asked him. "And ask the coroner to come down. There's something I need to look for."

After slowly working his way down the stairs, the coroner stood behind Alfano.

"Yes?"

"There's something I need to look for, and it may be behind the gag," Alfano told him. "Could you remove it and see if there is anything in his mouth?"

"Like earlier?"

"Just look."

The coroner looked closely at the gag and with a knife cut it through near the kid's cheek, leaving the knot in place. He removed the cloth and with his small flashlight peered into the open mouth. A piece of cloth was visible.

"And what do we have here," he said, as he firmly grasped the corner of the cloth with his surgical pliers and slowly pulled. When extracted, he unrolled the fabric.

"What the hell?" the captain said.

"It's the fascist flag, also found at the other murders," replied Alfano. "It seems to be a calling card."

"They don't seem to care who knows, do they?"

"No," Alfano said. "Pass the flashlight over the hand. I see something."

The light moved from the face to the arms and hands. On the back of the left hand, Alfano noticed a bluish tinge that stood out from the blood. It was in the shape of two letters: a capital L next to a capital O.

O'Malley looked over Alfano's shoulder and said, "Lo?"

"L and O," Alfano corrected him. "It's the hand stamp they use at Club Lola on State Street, a block from the Grand. The stamp lets you in and out after you pay the cover. It is, as they say in our line of work, a clue. And it's also finally a fucking place to start."

11

LUCCA BARONE climbed the steps up from his basement apartment and adjusted the strap on his shoulder satch-
el. He had two classes this morning, English language, then
American history. He lit a cigarette and headed to the elevated
rail line that would take him downtown. Only a few months
more, he told himself, then home. He missed the food more
than anything, and also his friends. These two he'd met in
Rome were okay, good chaps, but they also carried chips on
their shoulders. They all hated the fascists, each with their own
reasons, but Matteo and Sal held a visceral hatred, something
neither talked about. Even on the boat to America and over
subsequent dinners, they hadn't talked about their reasons for
this, as Sal called it, 'political action' against Mussolini.

"We have our orders," Sal said. "Without them we would
be rotting in some fascist Roman jail, so take advantage of
the situation and enjoy. All we have to do is this one simple
operation, then that's it. Hell, Lucca, if you like it here so much
after we are done, stay. Find some good-looking dame and get
married. All that asshole Mussolini will do to Italy is get us in a
war, we will get drafted, and die in some fucking hole in Ethi-
opia or Libya. Sal Rizzo has no intention of doing either and
neither does Cavallo here."

"Communists," Lucca said aloud, to no one in particular. *No better than the fucking fascists.*

He'd met the two at a small party given by one of the professors at the university. Only later had he found out that such parties were a recruiting opportunity for the communists. As a boy, he remembered his father telling him about America and the bounty that filled the country from one ocean to another. He also remembered an uncle on his mother's side, Uncle Pietro, who was funny and always bought him gelato as they walked the streets of Rome. One day Pietro had disappeared. He was never seen again, and it wasn't until Lucca was ten years old that he learned Pietro had been drafted into the army and killed on some war-blasted mountain north of Trieste. It was a brutal fight that took many fathers and brothers. The family had never learned where Pietro was buried.

Lucca knew why they wanted him in the party—it was because of his father's money or at least access to it. His father seemed to know what was happening and gave some tacit support through small cash donations as well as deposits into Lucca's personal accounts. Lucca and his father had never openly discussed Lucca's involvement with the communist party; all Lucca was told was to be very careful. He knew that his father despised Mussolini and the fascists, but his father's position in the Rome banking community required silence and secrecy. The university communists forgave Lucca for his less-than-ardent attitude regarding the opposition to Mussolini.

Now Lucca sat waiting in a small café on the eastern end of Taylor Street, smoking and sipping a cup of espresso. Class wouldn't start until ten o'clock, and she was late. He'd met Maria at a Loyola function. She was an Italian girl and the sister of one of his new American classmates. Lucca had been dating her for a few months, nothing serious yet; both were twenty-one and well past the usual stages of teenage romance. She was looking for something more, a partner and husband. He was looking for something more than the daily rants against the fascists by his Roman friends. He and Maria would talk for hours about jazz, baseball, and the fair. Maria DeRosa was working in the Italian exhibit. She gave lectures on Italian culture. Many Americans held Italians in low regard, fueled by the criminal activities of the likes of Al Capone, Frank Nitti and the Mafia. With the pending repeal of Prohibition, American attitudes had begun to change. Maria's job was to speak about the wealth of cultural contributions made by the Italians—not just the side of the Italian community shown in well-attended Hollywood gangster movies, but the arts and music as well.

Lucca watched her walk up the street toward the café. She was wearing her costume, really more of a peasant's dress and blouse that reminded him of small villages high in the Apennines to the east of Rome. In his less-than-worldly experience, she was absolutely beautiful. When she walked into the café, every man's eyes turned toward her. She strode directly to Lucca's table and sat.

"Sorry. Mother was a little under the weather, and I had to make sure my younger brother ate his breakfast and headed in the right direction to school, and I had to make father's lunch pail and I certainly could use one of those."

She pointed to the espresso cup.

"You're acting like you had three already," Lucca said.

"I wish. So be a good boy, would you?"

Lucca signaled to the café owner, who smiled, pointed at the espresso machine and held up one finger; one minute.

"You look *spettacolare* this morning, even after all the work you have already put in," he told Maria. "Your mother—it isn't serious, is it?"

"No, just the usual stomach issues, and this heat has not helped. She will be fine."

The owner placed a small cup on the table, and Maria lifted it to her lips and sipped. Unlike most men, who quickly shot back the caffeine-rich coffee, she savored each small taste.

"I have next Saturday night off. Do you think we can have dinner somewhere?" she asked Lucca. "Nothing fancy, but nice and for heaven's sake, not Italian."

"I think I can manage a night away from my studies, especially for a wench from a small mountainside village lost in this big city."

"It is your job to help this poor girl find her way home?"

"Sober?"

"And yes, Lucca Barone, sober. I have an early morning Sunday at the fair. So yes, sober."

Lucca smiled. Neither of them were drinkers, maybe a glass of wine with dinner but little else. Maria had seen too much liquor-induced damage done to her neighborhood, and while she supported the repeal of Prohibition, she also supported its failed lofty goals.

Lucca walked her to the trolley that took visitors and staff to the World's Fair; she kissed him on the cheek.

"I will call you at home just to confirm, okay?" he said.

"Don't tell my mother where we are going. I will tell her. And I will also let father know. You know how he is about my dating."

"You're over twenty-one."

"To him, I'm still fourteen, but I think he is beginning to like you."

"Ignoring me the whole time I'm there makes it hard to tell."

"Just be patient."

Patience was all he had these days, that and two dozen five-gallon cans of gasoline in his apartment. He headed north to class.

CARLA ACERBI parked the car in the basement stall

and quickly headed up the back stairs to her apartment. She had washed much of the blood from her hands before she left the man's house. She also carefully wiped every surface and doorknob she might have touched. She was methodical from beginning to end.

The list of Italian names she'd acquired from the university admissions office was long; she'd successfully used every method to sway the woman behind the counter to accommodate her request, even providing free tickets to the fair. The list was a mixture of both American Italians and recent students from Rome. Comparing to the given names extracted from the DeAngelos, the list contained four Luccas, two Salvatores, and three—well, now two—Matteos.

The first Matteo had been listed as a student, living in an apartment on Chicago's North Side, near the Loyola campus. For a day, she'd watched his apartment and eventually tailed him when he picked up his mail. She followed him that evening and sat five rows behind him on the south-bound 'L' train. As he quick-stepped down the stair from the platform, she held back and watched as he crossed State Street and headed toward a bar called Lola's. The neon letters flashed off and on over the line of jazz fans lining the street. The marquee overhead announced *Lux Lewis – Boogie-Woogie* in heavy black letters set against the brilliant white of the backlit sign. Matteo walked to the head of the line and spoke with the bouncer, who lifted the rope and let the man in.

He has pull. She crossed the street and stepped to the head of the line outside the club. Dressed in elegant slacks, white blouse with black dots, thin black linen jacket, and a cocked gray fedora, Acerbi leaned in close to the bouncer's ear and said in Italian, "I'm with Matteo." She didn't know if he understood completely, but he raised the rope and inclined his head toward the door.

The first two couples in line began to beef: "What the hell?

Who the fuck are they?"

"They are not you, so fuck off," the bouncer said.

He motioned to the couple immediately behind the four-some and waved them in.

"Goddamn it," the taller of the white kids said and moved toward the bouncer. In less time than needed to take a breath, the bouncer produced a small baseball bat and waved it in the youth's face.

"Not tonight, do you understand? Another step and you will be French kissing this fucker. Got it?"

The kid and his friends backed away.

"Screw this," one of them said. "Let's head to the Grand. The drinks are better there anyway."

Inside, Acerbi paid the two-dollar cover and held out her hand to be stamped. The sound of a piano and a brush slapping against a snare drum carried over the low din of conversation. She pushed through the crowd, scanning the room for Matteo; he stood alone next to the bar, a glass of beer in his hand. She thought for a moment then walked directly to him, a smile leading the way.

"Don't you go to Loyola," she said, looking at the young man. "I think I've seen you there on the campus. Someone said Matteo was your name."

Matteo looked at Acerbi and smiled back.

"Yeah to both counts. Bova is the last name. And you are?"

"Donna Delucca. Got a fag?"

Matteo produced a pack and shook one out to her. He clicked open his lighter, liking what he saw when the flame lit up her face.

"Haven't seen you here before," he said.

"I came in from Rome to help with the fair.

"Drink?"

Acerbi smiled and nodded. This was even easier than expected. Sipping the beer Matteo ordered for her, she watched the small combo with its boogie-woogie piano man pick up the tempo. In seconds the small dance floor was full. It was then that she noticed that she and Bova were in the minority; most of the patrons were black.

Bova pointed with his beer to a small table that had just cleared. She nodded again.

Conversation was almost impossible, especially when a tenor sax man took a seat next to the drummer. Acerbi's head began to pound from the smoke and incessant beat. She admitted to herself the beat was infectious, but listening to music wasn't her goal on this night. Luckily, before long the band took a break.

"Thanks for the beer," she said to Bova.

"It's okay. In a few months, all this Prohibition crap will be over. It's all been so foolish. Then real liquor."

He touched his glass to hers.

"The fair? I was there opening weekend. It's quite a sight, I'll tell you."

He asked Acerbi what her role was. She repeated the script she'd prepared about trying to find Italians who would add authenticity to the exhibits and act as theatrical actors and interpreters. She'd been a little surprised, she said, upon seeing a good-looking Italian when she came into Lola's.

"My gain," Bova answered.

"And mine as well."

It was Bova's idea to take the 'L' to the North Side. Her nibbling his ear after another drink most probably helped him to suggest the thought.

"I have a place we can use if you are interested. Very quiet and very private, if you know what I mean."

His smile was as lecherous as a twenty-one-year-old could make it.

"Do you have roommates?"

"No, no. My mother is away for a few days, visiting my

uncle. The place is all mine for now. Okay?"

"Well, I guess so," Acerbi said. "But we just met."

"Then it's a better chance to get to know each other, and this way we will have the whole night."

She nodded. They would indeed.

12

ALFANO pinned three of the photos from the Matteo Bova crime scene on the board. The similarities to the DeAngelos' murder were chilling, even for seasoned cops.

"Jesus," McDunnah said, as he studied the newest pictures. "And to think a woman is doing this? Damnation, if that's it, she's one seriously screwed-up broad."

McDunnah had rolled a blackboard next to the corkboard. He chalked a line down the middle. On the left, he wrote 'Suppositions,' and on the right, 'Facts.' Alfano jotted a few lines in his notebook, then looked back at the boards.

"She's looking for something," he said. "Each one of these people was brutally tortured, and because she's back here in Chicago, we can assume she hasn't found out what she wants or needs. All the victims are Italians. I'm not sure that's important, but let's put it on the right side."

They added to the lists, with Alfano occasionally consulting his notes and McDunnah writing on the board. On the left went possible traits: looking for something, probably a woman, lives in Chicago. On the right, all the knowns: all victims Italian, recent immigrants, all tortured, all strangled. Their goal was to move items from the left side to the right, as their various speculations were borne out by the investigation.

Alfano lit a cigarette, removed a large envelope from his lower desk drawer and opened it to take out a length of rope. He placed it next to the rope sample he'd retrieved from the Bova basement. As far as he could tell, they were both from the same coil. The ropes were slick, about three-eighths-inch thick, white, one end crisply cut with a very sharp knife and the other end frayed.

"What do you think this rope's made of, Sergeant?"

McDunnah rolled one of the cords in his fingers.

"Silk."

"Figures, a woman would use silk."

"Big supposition, yeah, but probable," McDunnah said.

"We searched every inch of the house and basement," Alfano added. "Nothing was out of the ordinary. If Mrs. Bova hadn't had a row with her brother and come home early, the body would still be undetected. He hadn't been dead twenty-four hours, according to the coroner."

"Neighbors didn't see anything?"

"Nothing so far, but O'Malley's men are still canvassing the street. Someone might have been up when Bova and the killer arrived at the house. The back of Bova's hand had a Lola's stamp. The place doesn't open until five, but I'll check it out then."

"These came when you were out," said McDunnah.

He handed Alfano three notes.

"The top one is the most important, the mayor."

"Just what I need."

Alfano looked at the clock over the entry and expected that His Honor would be back from lunch by now. He dialed the number for the mayor's office.

"Detective Anthony Alfano here. I'm returning the mayor's call. . . . Yes, that's correct, the call from this morning."

Alfano crushed out the end of his cigarette and lit another as he waited.

"Yes, sir," answered Alfano, reflexively sitting straighter in his chair when the mayor came on the line. He waited as the mayor went through all the protocols of sympathy over the events of the past month; much of which the mayor was, directly and indirectly, responsible for. The decision to keep one man on the city payroll had cost more than a dozen people their lives. Nevertheless, as a politician, the mayor declined to acknowledge that he had any responsibility, preferring to view the hideous events as the result of the bomber's deranged behavior.

"Yes, it is beginning to look like we have four victims, two here and two in Wisconsin," Alfano said, when the mayor asked about the current murders. "Same MO best we can tell, torture and strangulation. . . . Yes, I understand."

Alfano hung up.

"And how is that Irish sot?"

McDunnah set a fresh mug of coffee on Alfano's desk.

"He wants absolutely no reports in the press. He thinks it might affect attendance at the fair if there's a rumor that a killer is out there on the loose."

"I can see his point."

ALFANO drove south on State Street until he hit 30th Street. The red bricks that had once paved the great thoroughfare poked up through the asphalt, creating a crisscross pattern of patches and potholes. Trash and debris from the previous night's partygoers, high hats, and drunks littered the sidewalk and gutter. Jazz, hookers, and State Street didn't look good in daylight. The street came alive at night, when the swells and their money showed up and the neon letters hanging from the building parapets were turned on so that a million white lights shone on the street. For the next fifteen blocks, Alfano passed some of the best New Orleans jazz, boogie-woogie, and blues clubs flanking the street. In the humid morning, their signs hung cold and dark. He pulled to the curb and lit a cigarette while he waited. After a time, a distinguished-looking black man in a dark suit arrived and began placing one letter after another on the marquee of the Regal. Some nights, musicians with instruments in hand would stroll back and forth across South State Street, playing from one joint to another. Names like the Grand Terrace Ballroom, the Cabin Inn, the Regal, the Red Mill, Dreamland Café and the Oriental Café lined the street like well-lacquered whores waving come-ons at the Johns. The likes of Jelly Roll Morton, Louis Armstrong, Grover Compton and Earl "Fatha" Hines played State Street. In spite of the gangs and Prohibition, State Street had survived—and for five of its headier years, it had been Alfano's beat as a patrolman. The denizens of the street knew him, and he knew them.

He moved his car up to 35th Street and parked in the alley-way behind Lola's. The heat was rising and with it the stench from the backstreet that split the block between Dearborn and State. He walked down the alley to Lola's; the door was open. There were no lines out front, no bouncer, and no patrons inside—yet. A solitary man stood at the bar, cleaning glasses. The soft sounds of a piano's ruminations, tinkled by a young black woman, filled the otherwise empty club.

"Well I'll be fucked this Sunday after church, if it isn't Tony Alfano?" the bartender said. "I haven't seen you in more than a year."

"Almost two, Clarence, almost two years. If I remember right, it was after that fellow from Jackson, Mississippi, was shot in the alley. Over a woman wasn't it?"

Clarence smiled.

"Isn't it always about a woman? Yeah, if I remember, the cracker got his own ass shot up a week later. Street justice, what can you say. . . . We miss you down here."

"I've been meaning to drop by—good times here. Only

six more months, then all this liquor silliness will be over."

"I'm counting the days, Tony. But we're all legit here with beer and wine, I can tell you that."

"I'll take your word for that, Clarence, as always."

"You're jake, Alfano. A guy can always count on a square deal. It's a little early for a drink, so I guess you're here for information."

Alfano laid a picture on the bar. It was a headshot of Matteo Bova.

"Dead?"

"Very, and not nicely. Know him?"

"I've seen him around here the past six months. He's not a regular but comes for the tunes and maybe some of the girls. Young kid, a bit randy, likes chocolate."

"Was he here this week?"

Clarence studied the photo again.

"Yes, maybe two nights ago. Wanda, get your skinny ass over here."

The piano stopped and its player walked to the bar. Alfano studied her walk and the forced grace of her style, the way she used her hands to balance herself. She was high on something.

"Wanda here was working the floor. You see this guy a couple of nights ago?"

The thin woman studied the photo, pushed it forward and back on the bar top, like she was snaking a small trombone.

"Yeah, this kid's made a pass at me a few times," she told the two men. "He drank only beer. But the son of a bitch wasn't interested in what I had that night, no siree. Had this big bitch of a white woman with him. They came in separate-like. Sat over there."

She pointed.

"Can you describe her?" Alfano asked.

"My memory is a little hazy," she said.

"Wanda, you tell Tony here what he needs, and don't try to

boost him up for a five. There are ten girls wanting your job, so fucking tell him."

Alfano wasn't sure what he'd get; Wanda's eyes kept focusing in and out, but she thought for a few seconds and then gave better details than most people would have sober.

"She was very tall for a dago, then again, everyone's taller than little ol' me. Good looking in a hard, bitchy sort of way. Dark hair, cut short, modern-like, combed back, greased. She dressed like a pimp I once knew: dark suit, white open collar, a manly look about her. Diamond studs in the ears; shit, might have even been real."

"You sure she was Italian?"

"Yeah, guess so."

Wanda asked Clarence for some water. She took a sip and then lit a cigarette.

"She was kind of strange, definitely stood out in a place like this. You know, a white guy and broad show up."

"He comes for the music—I mean, he came for the music," said Clarence.

"He dead?" Wanda asked.

"Yes, murdered," Alfano replied.

"She have something to do with it?"

"Maybe."

"Fuck. She looked like the type who'd cut your throat for the fun of it."

"That's an interesting way to put it. Was there anything else? What made you think she's Italian?"

"That's the lingo the two of them spoke. I knows it from some kids I grew up with."

"He also bought a bottle of whiskey, a small pint. The last one I had," Clarence said, with a smile.

"Last one, how lucky."

Clarence tapped the photo with his finger.

"Yeah, lucky for me and unlucky for this poor son of a bitch."

13

MARIA DEROSA took her usual spot in the main lobby of the Italian pavilion, a large antique wicker basket used to carry flowers tucked under one arm. Today the basket was full of brochures advertising the fair and the pavilion. She strolled among the visitors, answering questions and, more often than not, pointing the way to the restrooms. While not glamorous, the job did give her a chance to meet people and talk about the exciting events coming later in the summer and most especially the arrival of Italo Balbo and his squadron. In celebration of Italy's aerospace industry, the pavilion was shaped like a giant airplane and the vertical architectural tower in the front was a modern replica of a Roman lictor's rods and mace. It was also the symbol of the Italian fascist party.

Posters of the coming event filled the walls of the lobby; a small replica of one of the seaplanes was featured in an exhibit in the atrium. In fact, she had learned, there were other Italian exhibits in the Hall of Science, Adler Planetarium, and even the Museum of Science and Industry. Her supervisor had said that Maria would be working those exhibits later in the summer. It was thrilling for a simple Chicago girl, and her parents bragged about her job at the pavilion. Maria had been told that the staff were preparing a marble column shipped from

Italy that Mussolini had given to celebrate Balbo's flight. The two-thousand-year-old column from the port of Ostia would be unveiled the day Balbo was to arrive. Unfortunately, no one could tell exactly when that would be. The weather would play a critical yet bothersome role in the schedule. The latest rumor that morning was mid to late July. The radio announcement that the squadron had left Italy had suddenly changed everything; there was a palpable excitement growing in the pavilion.

"*Posso fare una domanda?*" a voice said from behind Maria. She turned.

"My Italian is not so good but yes, you may ask me a question," she responded.

"Oh, that's okay, my English isn't too bad. I thought all of you were required to speak Italian," the woman said.

Maria had to look up at the woman's face.

"Some of us are better," Maria said. "I'm second generation—makes a difference. Do you wish to speak with someone more fluent?"

"No, you will do. I am trying to find the pavilion's office. I have some questions, and I was told they might have some of the answers."

"Maybe I can help, Signorina . . ."

"Donna Delucca. I'm from Rome, on a holiday as well as on official business regarding the arrival of General Balbo."

"Oh, my, isn't this exciting? It will be wonderful. So many of my friends can hardly wait. You are involved?" Maria asked, astounded by her good fortune.

"Only in a small way—some preparations for the crew's accommodations and transportation when they arrive. Small stuff. My staff is handling those things."

"Well, the office is down that hallway to the rear. Just follow the signs."

"Thank you, Miss . . ."

"DeRosa. Maria DeRosa."

"I will mention how helpful you've been, Miss DeRosa. It is a compliment to our country that even here, thousands of miles from our homeland, there are people who still believe in Italy and its future."

The woman smiled and placed her fingers against Maria's cheek.

"Yes, and you are a pretty young thing."

Maria unexpectedly recoiled from the touch. It was almost instinctive, as if she'd been touched with a live wire. She watched the woman turn and head down the hallway. Maria felt chilled, even in the warmth of the morning. She had never met a woman like Donna Delucca; she didn't understand it, but it frightened her. She was now thanking herself for not mentioning that her boyfriend's name was Lucca, the root of Signorina Delucca's name. Yes, for some unexplainable reason, she was glad she had not made the comment.

AFTER a short meeting at the pavilion's offices, Acerbi sat on one of the benches that overlooked the great lagoon centered in the fairgrounds. She smiled at the thought of the young woman in the atrium. Yes, quite cute, even sweet. Her naiveté reminded Acerbi of the DeAngelo girl. She blinked slowly to clear her head—back to business. After killing Bova, she needed to find a faster and more focused way to go through the list of names from the university. The current method was taking too long and was potentially too random; she had wasted three days setting up Bova. The right Matteo could be the next one on the list or the last; only if she were lucky would she find the right three students in time. A telegram sent from Rome the day before had indicated that the squadron of planes would leave Italy on Sunday—today. Considering the time difference, General Italo Balbo and his squadron of twenty-four seaplanes were now in the air on their way to Amsterdam. They would take about ten days to reach Chicago. The clock had started.

Carla Acerbi had met Italo Balbo once, at a training center in the Apennines. He'd been cordial, almost warm, in his conversations with the men and women at the camp. He spoke of the high regard he and the Prime Minister had for their work and their selfless ideals for the state and the party. She followed his career as both a fascist political leader and his development of the Italian air force into one of the finest in the world. His first crossing of the Atlantic Ocean, from Italy to Brazil, three years earlier, was still talked about. Flying was still wondrous and at the same time frightful to the uneducated peasants in the hills of Italy. She'd seen the airplanes—all designed and built by Italians, her Italians—at the airport north of Rome. All were magnificent machines of aluminum, wood and steel. To think that in just over a week someone could travel from Rome to Chicago was astounding. When Acerbi was born, it would have taken more than a month, maybe longer, on a combination of boats and trains to accomplish what the general and his men now did in a week. She also knew that ideas could now travel even faster; the telegram in her hand proved that.

The men she hunted were in this city and, from what the DeAngelos had divulged, were entirely on their own. There was no one in the city to help them and, subsequently, no one to turn them over to the authorities.

"Signore Barbieri, I need your help," she had said to the man standing at the window of the small back office of the Italian pavilion.

"Yes? Help? You?" the man answered.

He was dressed in a custom-made linen suit—she guessed Milan—and black-and-white shoes. His silk tie favored the colors of the Italian flag yet with a subtle collage of shapes. He held a cigarette in a holder; the smoke rose and reflected off the monocle over his right eye. His nose, pockmarked and discolored, was bent to the left.

"You need my help?"

"Yes, I have found that there are three suspects."

"And you found this out, how?"

"Not your concern," she snapped. "These three have legally come into this country during the last four months. Here are their first names."

She placed a paper on the desk. Barbieri walked to the desk and with two fingers rotated the sheet so he could read it.

"I need you and your offices here in this country to find out their last names and where they live. They must have reported to someone; your people in the American government can help."

"What makes you think I have people in the government?"

"With all the comings and goings and deportations of convicted Mafioso during the last fifteen years, I'm sure you have sources in both Immigration and in the courts. I need these names, and I needed them yesterday."

"So, I'm doing your job?"

"You would piss in your pants if you did my job. Trouble is, I don't have time to do *your* job. Find these people and send me the information. You know where to leave it."

He looked down at the woman who had casually taken a seat at the desk; he had seen her type before in some of the trendier bars and clubs in Milan, clubs quietly favored by some members of the party.

"There are reports of unfortunate deaths among members of the Italian community here in the Chicago region," he said.

"And you are concerned? Why?"

"I do not wish to have the Americans again looking into the affairs of the Italian government. We have been very cooperative with their World's Fair, and now that this Prohibition is coming to an end, we are hoping to export some of our wine to this country. We can't have the Americans just drinking French wine, can we?"

"I really don't care. You are like every other politician I've known—one moment concerned about the deaths of people you don't know and the next about money. Maybe the communists are correct about you and some members of the party."

Barbieri crushed his cigarette into an ashtray, pulled the stub from the holder and inserted another cigarette he took from a gold case on the desk.

"Our concern is the reputation of Italy, don't you forget it. That is the reason you are here, to prevent an embarrassment. You are not here for your, how should I put this, your personal pleasures. We know about you."

Acerbi smiled.

"Then you know what I'm capable of. I am your instrument, Signore Barbieri, yours and the prime minister—I accept that role. I have my assignment and, as you well know, I always finish my assignments. How I accomplish that has not been questioned—until now."

She paused and looked at the rat of a man before her.

"Are you now questioning me?"

It was Barbieri's turn to smile.

"Such games we play, Signorina Acerbi. Go, I will find your names, and you will have your toys. In ten days, this will all be over. And that means you have ten days to resolve this . . . situation."

Acerbi returned to the corridor and went out a narrow doorway in the rear of the building, exiting into the massive crowd that filled the fairgrounds. Beyond, Lake Michigan extended north to the horizon.

14

SAL RIZZO and Matteo Cavallo spent the afternoon walking through Lincoln Park on the near North Side. Earlier they had strolled through the park's zoo, even fed the monkeys. Afterward, they headed farther along the lakefront of Lake Michigan to the North Lagoon, one of the larger inlets built along the reclaimed land that had once been Chicago's first cemetery. The two Italians admired the motor launches and sailboats tied to buoys scattered about the protected cove that connected directly to the lake. Small dinghies and other craft used to ferry the boat owners to their crafts were secured to a short pier; others were pulled up on the narrow, sandy beach.

Sal lit a cigar.

"Any of those will do nicely," he offered in Italian. "That one there, says *Blackhawk* on its bow, would be perfect."

The boat had *Racine* printed on its stern—"wherever that is," he added. "It may mean the owners are not local. That would make it easier to steal. She looks fast and certainly can carry what we need."

"How the hell are we going to get those cans of gasoline on board that boat?" Matteo wanted to know.

Like Lucca, he was becoming increasingly uncomfortable with the operation.

"We certainly can't load those small boats, row out there, and then do it again and again. This whole idea is fucked. What did they think we could do?" he said.

"Our job! The way I figure it, we will come down here during the festivities celebrating the fascist's triumphant flight into Chicago. No one watches these boats. We row out and slowly move the boat out of the harbor. Then go south around Navy Pier and up the Chicago River. There are dozens of places we can tie up and load the cans onboard. I found a good location under the Harrison Street Bridge. Once loaded, we head back out. Balbo will be here at least two days and nights. We will have plenty of time."

"We don't even know where they will be."

"They are fucking seaplanes. They will be on the water, you idiot. That's why we are here looking at these boats."

Sal tossed his cigar into the lagoon.

"We are going to do this, do you understand? That bastard Mussolini has to know that we will attack him anywhere we want. Nowhere is safe. We are almost there. No one will expect this; hell, the papers are calling Balbo a hero and the asshole hasn't even landed yet. We can work out the details later. From what I've read, it will take them seven or eight days to get here, and that's with good weather. My guess, even longer, meaning we will have time to go over this again and again. We will get it right, and more importantly, no one will catch us."

Matteo didn't say anything; he just stood on the lakeshore and looked at the dozens of motor launches moored in the lagoon.

Yes, it might work, we might succeed and yes, it could be disastrous for the fascists. But then again it might be a fucking deadly disaster—for us.

ANTHONY ALFANO was not pleased by the call from the mayor—save the fool's job once and he was a friend for life. Edward Kelly, the mayor of Chicago for less than two months, after his predecessor, Anton Cermak, had been assassinated, now had the whole world neatly placed in his lap with the opening of the Century of Progress World's Fair. He was there for the ribbon cutting and there with his cronies for the opening of any new pavilion. Alfano was sure he would show up at the exhibit on the fair's Midway, which would be filled with newly born babies, so he could be the first to kiss one. The man was a pompous ass and a political hack, but he was also Alfano's boss.

Life was never fucking fair.

However, the real reason Alfano despised the man was because Kelly had been directly responsible for Gini's death.

After additional canvassing of the Bova neighborhood, police found one man who'd noticed a cab dropping two people off on the street where Bova lived. Bova had looked a little "tight," but the man was sure the cab was a Checker.

"Nooo doubt about," he'd said. "Drove for them five years ago, then was dumped when the crash came. All capitalistic bastards, and that's the nice stuff I can call them. Yes, sure as hell, it was a Checker."

McDunnah made a call and set in motion the cab company's search of its records from that night. He had both ends of the trip with the information Alfano had obtained from Lola's and where the hack had ended up. Two hours later, his phone rang.

McDunnah scribbled down notes and the cab's number.

"He driving now? . . . Have him stop by the Racine Station. . . . Don't give me excuses; this is part of a murder investigation. I want him here in less than an hour."

McDunnah slammed the receiver onto its hook. Shortly after, the cabbie, one Timothy Doolan, stood twisting his cap in his hands outside the station entrance, looking left and right, not sure if he should go in. McDunnah helped by opening the station door.

"You Doolan? Good, get your ass in here. You're not in trouble; we just have some questions. Go, there."

He pointed to a room off the lobby.

"Coffee?"

Doolan nodded and headed in the direction McDunnah pointed.

Alfano looked at the man sitting at the steel desk in the interview room. It was easy to tell that he'd not had much contact with the police. The man was nervous, not the shaky, guilty type of nervous, but the *what the hell did I do?* type.

McDunnah brought in coffee. Doolan nodded his thanks and took a sip. He did not please McDunnah with a smile; it was more of a grimace.

"I don't like it either," the sergeant said.

Alfano introduced himself.

"You're here because you may be the last person, other than his killer, to see this man alive."

He showed Doolan the same photo of Bova that he'd shown to Clarence at Lola's.

"You were just doing your job, no problems. But we are trying to get a lead on what happened. You picked up this fare on 35th last Wednesday night and took him to this address."

Alfano laid another piece of paper on the table.

"Tell us what happened."

Timothy Doolan looked at the photo and the paper with the address written on it.

"This guy dead?" he asked.

"Yes, viciously murdered," Alfano said.

"Jesus. What about the woman?"

"What woman?" McDunnah said, trying to draw out Doolan.

"He was with this sharp-looking broad, Italian to be sure—a knockout. My first call was that she was out of his league, but I don't make judgments. Been driving too long to do that. I get's all types in the cab—as I said, she was a looker. She snuggled up close the whole time. Yeah, I thought he was too young for her, that's why I remember."

He took another sip of coffee and looked at McDunnah.

"Grows on you," he said.

"Like rust. What else?" McDunnah asked.

"It was a long ride, maybe twenty minutes. When I pulled up to the street, she said to just stop at the corner. They'd walk. The kid just nodded. Couldn't hold his liquor, I guess."

"What else?"

"I thought he'd picked up a hooker, but she paid. The fare was over ten bucks—made my night. Then she walked him up the street to a house two or three from the corner. I passed them as she was getting him up the steps. That's all I know."

"Describe her," Alfano said.

"Italian for sure, dark hair, well built and good looking, maybe five-seven or eight. A few inches taller than that guy."

He pointed to the picture of Bova.

"All the girls out that night had on light summer dresses," he said. "But she wore a woman's suit, looked more like a guy than a gal. Carried herself well, business-like, even when she was tuning up the kid."

"Tuning up?"

"Yeah, making sure he kept taking swigs from a bottle he had. It worked; he was almost out when she got him to the front door."

"You catch a name?"

"He mumbled something like Lana, Ranna. No, Donna. It was Donna. No last name, but sure as hell, he called her Donna."

15

THE GREATEST EVENT the city of Chicago had embraced in more than thirty years now fully involved almost every man, woman and child in the city. Thousands of Chicagoans worked at the Century of Progress World's Fair, and tens of thousands passed through its entry gates each day. Four years into the Depression that wracked the country and much of the civilized world, Chicago fended it off, like a prizefighter bobbing and weaving, hoping the contender doesn't land a lucky punch. The fair's jobs were its biggest benefit and the spin-off cab drivers, hotel maids, waitresses, and even hookers added to the welcome exchange of hard currency for services and entertainment.

Alfano was also sure the event would attract more than tourists. His twenty years on the force had shown him time and again that where there was an itch—for booze, sex, gambling—there would be those to help scratch it. He'd already seen an increase in his district of drunkards rolled for their bankrolls, hookers messed up on cocaine and weed, and plain old strong-arming of tourists who ventured outside of their hotels. And now these Italian murders. He'd thought, actually wished, that these types of killings—Italians killing Italians as with Capone and the Outfit—were on the way out. Capone was rotting in prison somewhere near Atlanta. With liquor on the way to becoming legal again and rumors that the over-all economy was getting better, even though he hated rumors, he'd grown hopeful. Now, with these new killings, he wasn't sure.

McDunnah came over to pin another of his crude sketches to the board. He dropped a small bag on Alfano's desk.

"Your drawing skills need improving, and what's this?" Alfano said.

"It's obviously the outline of a head—that's our killer. If I knew the name of a good-looking Italian actress, I'd put that up there. However, under that well-drawn outline are the statistics we've collected. From those I expect there are maybe a few hundred women here in Chicago that fit the description."

Alfano nodded. Despite his quirks, the sergeant was his best ally on the job.

"The bag has some poppers and firecrackers—a little something to you from me for the holiday," McDunnah said. "The missus wants to know if you'll join us for the Fourth of July. We're doing a block party, good food, a small jazz combo, and some Irish lads from Dublin will be playing. From the end of our street, we will have a view of the fireworks from the fair."

Alfano thought for a moment.

"Sure beats staying in my hot apartment," he said. "Time?"

"Midafternoon. She'll be glad to see you."

McDunnah looked back at the board.

"Not sure we are any closer than we were a week ago," he said thoughtfully.

"Waiting for another body—that's just not right. Let's look at what this is not."

McDunnah nodded, and they both studied the items on the board as Alfano outlined his ideas.

"Okay. We're not saying it's not gang related. Nothing

about any of these deaths puts the victims in the syndicates or the mob. The DeAngelo girl, working class, naive and vulnerable; the parents were immigrants, professionals, comfortable. Matteo Bova—he's the one I don't get. Nothing we have says that he even knew the DeAngelos. Not even from the same region. The DeAngelos are Roman; Bova was Sicilian."

"And how'd you know that?"

"Just do, like you know where the McCarthys and O'Tooles come from. We know that names have regional roots, some even based on spellings. I know Italians and you intuitively know the Irish. It's an educated guess, but we're still nowhere closer. For now, let's agree it's a woman, that she is seriously looking for something or someone. She kills easily and with a distinct and repetitive pattern."

"In some ways, it's like a gangland hit," McDunnah said. "Assassin, hired killer?"

"Yeah, maybe. Go with me on this. Why is she searching? Who's she looking for? Question one: has she been hired to do a job finding someone or something? Two, was she hired for her skills? Three, her looks and sex allow her anonymity. No one would suspect her. She can act the part of the cute kitten before she turns into the throat-ripping lioness."

"That all works for me, Detective. Now where do we find such a cat?"

THE YEARNING, the ache, was visceral. It started low, like a warm spot in her abdomen, and expanded until it seemed to be all she could think of. The round bottom of a secretary walking along the sidewalk, the shake of a head of soft hair, even the ads in magazines—all seemed to trigger this need for intimacy, touching, probing and, above all else, the release and satisfaction.

From her vantage point near the 'L' on State Street on the night she'd followed Matteo Bova, she'd noticed something that only her kind would recognize. Four doors down from Lola's, a small bar had a dozen customers coming and going. To the quick and indifferent glance, it was just another night-club—like a dozen other nightspots in the neighborhood—with well-dressed patrons in gowns and tuxedos, swells and their dates. A flat, backlit sign near the door read *Toutou's*. As Carla Acerbi had passed the bar that night, two dozen sets of eyes had followed her.

"There's more fun in here, girl, than that dump Lola's," one of the patrons waiting in line out front of Toutou's had called out to her. The thin ghost of a black woman had blown smoke from a cigarette in a long ebony holder. "Yeah, girl, a lot more fun," she added, looking longingly after Acerbi.

Now, four days later, Acerbi pulled to the curb in front of Toutou's and waited behind another sedan as it emptied. Four striking and elegantly dressed black customers exited the car and stood at the curb as the valet handed the driver, who wore a svelte tuxedo, a claim ticket. One of the women in the group looked through Acerbi's windscreen and smiled. Then the valet, a wiry black kid in a worn tuxedo, quick-walked to Acerbi.

"Valet, Miss?"

"Yes, but keep it near," Acerbi said.

She handed the kid a five.

"Yes'um, I'll keep it real close."

This was not the first time he'd heard this simple order.

As were two of the women from the sedan, Acerbi was dressed in a conservative summer-weight tuxedo. She wore a tight undershirt that somewhat suppressed her ample bosom, giving a fuller manly look to her style. A black top hat, cocked to the left, finished the guise. She smiled at the bouncer at the door, who waved her in. A white woman was always welcome.

The club was loud, and the haze of a hundred cigarettes and cigars filled the narrow room. A long bar, with a dozen oc-cupied stools, lined the wall to the right of the entrance. Mirrors and very risqué French posters paneled the back bar. At a piano, located mid-club, sat a large black woman in a tuxedo; her fingers drove a rough and raunchy song of lost loves and affections. Acerbi elbowed her way through the crowd, more than once feeling a hand run its fingers and palm across her backside. She never looked, but the groping excited her.

A full-figured woman seated at the far end of the bar smiled and motioned her over.

"You're new here," the woman said, when Carla reached the bar. "Yes, new but not, how should I say, inexperienced. Cigarette?"

"No, thank you," Acerbi said, standing sideways at the bar so she could look over the crowd. "Yes, I'm visiting."

"Nice accent. It has a European touch to it. I lived in Paris six years ago. Yes, your accent is amusing, and I can tell it's real. Are you here with the fair?"

"Somewhat connected, but yes, the fair."

As she answered, Acerbi kept her gaze focused on the clubgoers. Some manly attired, others were very feminine and dressed in silks and shear fabrics. The patrons were surprisingly not unlike most nightclubs, other than the fact almost all were women.

"This is my place. I modeled it after a club in Paris," the woman said and motioned to the bartender. "I just love to help my new friends find—new friends. Are you in need of a friend?"

She blew a smoke ring.

"Very nice," Acerbi said, as she continued to look around the room, but the look was more of an inspection of the possibilities. "Yes, a friend would be nice."

"Yes, a friend," the bar owner said. "Two Camparis, Billie."

Billie was a tall, reed of a woman, short haircut, tight trousers, and white blouse with its sleeves and cuffs held in place with garters.

"Yes ma'am," she answered her boss.

"Nothing for me," Acerbi said.

"My dear, really? Your loss—just one."

Acerbi gave a slight shake of her head to the bartender, who moved away quickly.

"I'm Madame Marie," the club owner said, as she held out her hand. "Preferences? I can tell a woman who has decided preferences. Tall, thin, amply sized, manly or feminine? So many possibilities."

Acerbi released the woman's hand. The grip had been hard and long. Madame Marie would be formidable and pleasing, she thought—but too large for her tastes. The singer stopped playing and stood to the claps and applause of the crowd. She waved at the bartender, who raised a tall glass.

"The piano player is very good," Acerbi said, as she watched the young woman make her way through the crowd to the bar.

"She's taken."

"Only commenting on her playing, I lean toward more feminine and lanky.

"Don't we all. I've been watching. There are many eyes on you. May I ask your name?

"Donna Delucca," Acerbi said. "And I hadn't noticed."

"Miss Delucca, women of our type always notice."

16

SERGEANT MCDUNNAH lived in Bridgeport. The South Side neighborhood was the center of the Irish population in Chicago. Mixed in amongst the fifty thousand or so of McDunnah's countrymen were smatterings of immigrants from Poland and Eastern Europe. Catholic churches towered on almost every corner; one wondered where one parish ended and another began. The nearby stockyards and the Union Rolling Mills provided jobs, and the new Comiskey Park (built by a favorite Irish son, Charles Comiskey) provided recreation and was home to the White Sox. The neighborhood was also the birthplace and home of the Mayor Edward Kelly.

It was Kelly who ruined the Fourth of July afternoon for Alfano soon after the detective arrived to celebrate the holiday with his sergeant. Alfano was walking along the street with McDunnah, a beer in one hand and a Vienna Beef Red Hot in the other. It seemed to Alfano that every third person McDunnah introduced to him was either a cop or a fireman. He guessed that most of the others were on the city's payroll in one kind of a job or another. There was not a tighter knit neighborhood in Chicago.

The continuous snapping and crackling of fireworks and the yelling of the kids as they raced up and down the street provided the background to the real music that came from each end of the barricaded street. There was a Polish oompah band at one end and an Irish tenor at the other. While tickets weren't required, it was fairly obvious that you either had to know someone or live in the neighborhood to enjoy the festivities.

"Shit, why the hell is he here?" McDunnah said, when they saw the mayor. "I was hoping he'd find some other part of town to annoy. Most tolerate the SOB, but none would invite him in for a pint."

Alfano watched as Kelly and his small entourage of sycophants strolled through the crowd, shaking hands and rubbing kids heads.

Yes, why the hell is he here? And I was having such a good time.

By the time the mayor reached Alfano and McDunnah, the hot dog was gone and all Alfano had to hold was beer in a paper cup.

"Detective Alfano, what a pleasure to see you here," Kelly said, extending his hand. "I thought you lived north of here."

Alfano caught the implication: *This is Irish turf, my turf. What's a dago like you doing here?*

"I'm a guest of my sergeant, sir. Mayor, this is Sergeant McDunnah. He's the glue that holds our station together."

"Mayor, a pleasure," McDunnah said, and they shook hands.

McDunnah needed no introduction to Kelly. The man was a political legend to every Irish kid and an example of how to game the system for your friends and your community. No one said or did anything about the corruption—real or imagined—since many were direct recipients of the mayor and the city's largess. Now only in his tenth week as mayor, the citizens of Bridgeport expected a good measure from their current favorite son.

"Can you believe that General Balbo stopped in Ireland?

What a coup for us," Kelly said.

"I believe he's in Northern Ireland," Alfano said.

"Detective, we Irish believe in only one Ireland, not this unholy split to our country that the English have forced on us. Lord be praised, the bastards are out of most the old country. If I were younger, I'd go and help to finally throw them out."

"Yes, sir," Alfano said halfheartedly.

Standing behind the mayor, McDunnah could only shake his head.

Kelly leaned in toward Alfano and said, "Do you have a moment, Detective? I need a word."

Alfano nodded and the two of them walked a few paces away from the others.

"What the hell's going on, Alfano? There's been another murder—my people are saying by the same deranged person. Are there others, others you haven't found?"

"I don't know who *your* people are, but *I* haven't made a decision yet on who the killer is. Until then, it's all conjecture. And as to others, I haven't a fucking clue."

The mayor looked at Alfano as if what he meant to say next caught in his throat. Finally he said, "What do you know?"

Alfano briefed the mayor on what had been established about the suspect, including the growing certainty that the killer was female.

"I want this son of a bitch found, man or woman. Got it, Alfano? There's already some rumbling about this Bova kid from the press. How they got onto it, I don't know."

"The mother, sir."

"The mother?"

"Yes, sir. I understand the family went to the local Italian press with the story, hoping to find out who killed Bova. All it's done is mess up our investigation. We get crank calls, false leads. Hell, we even got another Matteo Bova in town whose mother thought he was the one murdered—a fucking mess."

A couple of young boys walked up to the mayor. One of the youths was holding a baseball. He offered it to the mayor along with a fountain pen.

"You want me to sign it?"

The boy nodded.

"First for me, Alfano. I've never signed a baseball before. Sure. I'll tell you, Alfano, before my mayoring days are over I'll be signing a lot of stuff, and a baseball might be the easiest. Here you go, boys."

Kelly looked east toward the high decks of Comiskey Park.

"You fellows practice and maybe you'll be playing in an All-Star Game someday," he told the boys.

The boys skipped off, and Kelly reached into his pocket and took out an envelope, which he handed to Alfano.

"These are for you and your sergeant—tickets to the game."

It was obvious the mayor loved being an Irish Santa Claus, handing out gifts and signatures. Alfano wondered what else he'd given away that day.

"You keep me informed, Detective. Anything you need from me, just call. I know you'll get to the bottom of this—I just don't want any more bodies."

The mayor's entourage moved on, stopping at a long table full of baked goods. Two nuns stood under a hand-lettered sign that read *Nativity of Our Lord Church*. The mayor pointed to a few buns and confections covered in frosting. The sisters pressed the bag of sweets into his hands.

Watching this, Alfano and McDunnah exchanged a wry glance.

"Everyone wants a favor, Detective, everyone," the sergeant said, his voice low so that only Alfano could hear.

AFTER the Fourth of July fireworks, Maria and Lucca sat on a blanket on the lawn in Grant Park, watching the newest and showiest addition to the Chicago lakefront, Buckingham Fountain, shoot great streams of water into the air.

"You look tired," Lucca said. "Is everything okay?"

"Other than being exhausted, I'm fine. The crowds were unbelievable today. They said that more than two hundred thousand people had come to the fair by late afternoon. Sometimes I thought they were all in my pavilion. I was lucky I had the early shift today. All I want to do is sleep."

Lucca stared out into the blackness of Lake Michigan. Dots of red, green, and white from the hundreds of navigation lights of the boats busied themselves on the water.

"Something is bothering you, I can tell," Maria said softly, as she gently stroked his cheek. "Can I help?"

Lucca took her hand in his and lowered it to his lap.

"Nothing I can talk about. Just some things at school— things I have to finish by the end of the term."

"Nothing to do with those two friends of yours, is it?"

"A little, but I can handle them."

Maria made a face.

"They're strange," she said, still frowning. "They can't even have a decent conversation about restaurants and the fair and all the exciting things that are happening in Chicago. For them, it's all politics. How the business owners and the companies are enslaving people, causing the depression to force wages down. . . . No, Lucca Barone, I do not like them one bit. But then again, my family would never have anything to do with the communists."

"And the fascists are better?"

"Don't you start; it has been too nice a day. But to answer your question, no, they are not any better. President Roosevelt is beginning to make some big changes that will help all of us. All without the foreign meddling of the communists and the fascists. What's happening in Europe right now is very troubling, but I have faith in Roosevelt."

"I don't know him like I do the fascists in my country. They are thugs and killers," Lucca replied, a trace of bitterness in his voice. "They have taken over every aspect of life in Italy. In many ways, being here in Chicago has helped me to understand my home better."

"And why are you here, not that I'm complaining, mind you? You can go to school anywhere. Your father is successful, there are no limits on what you can do—especially here."

He kissed her on the cheek and smiled.

"When you say it that way, I can almost see the future. But I have obligations that I need to deal with. Then we'll see if there is a future."

"That scares me. What are you talking about?"

Instead of answering, Barone rolled to his side and kissed Maria, this time on the lips. Even with the warm night, she snuggled close, deciding not to press him further, at least not now. They walked home; the streets and buses were jammed with late-night tourists and celebrators. Standing outside her apartment, Lucca said, "Tomorrow night?"

"I'm on from eight in the morning to six. Do you want to come over and have dinner?"

He smiled.

"Lasagna?"

"Yes, my mother made a tray. Say about seven? You bring the wine; I won't ask where you got it."

MARIA DEROSA had been a pleasant surprise. Barone was told before he left Rome to keep the Americans at arm's length. "Do not get involved," he was advised. "Be friendly, but be careful. They are too inquisitive and eventually will discover what you are doing." A classmate introduced Lucca to Maria at a small after-school event that neither of his co-conspirators attended. He immediately forgot most of what his communist professor had told him about Americans. He'd fallen, to use the local jargon, head over heels for the dark-eyed Italian, whose parents were successful restaurant owners on Chicago's near South Side. When his friends found out, they'd forbidden him from seeing her. He'd ignored them and now, months after their arrival, Cavallo and Rizzo had realized they couldn't dissuade Lucca from seeing the girl. Point of fact, the two were jealous of Lucca's good fortune and, after meeting her, more than taken by her beauty and charm. However, they continued to insist that Lucca be careful.

Barone was unsure what to do. He'd been caught up in the adventure, but now he was certain what he was doing was wrong. The gasoline, stored in his basement apartment, would cause a lot of damage if properly used, but he wasn't certain that any of them, especially Sal, knew what they were doing. There were times when Sal acted more like one of the fascist thugs they'd known in Rome. He wasn't in any of Lucca's classes, and when Lucca asked what courses he was taking, Sal never gave a straight answer. Lucca had privately come to the conclusion that Sal Rizzo was not even attending classes at Loyola.

Matteo Cavallo did attend some classes but never asked questions or for Lucca's help with studies. There were times when he thought Cavallo was there to just watch him. After the first week they were together, Maria had taken Lucca to see the new gangster movie, *Scarface*. Sitting in the dark theater, he began to believe that Sal Rizzo saw himself as the Paul Muni character and would stop at nothing to carry out the communists' plan. When this was all over, Lucca hoped that he and Maria wouldn't end up, like in the movie, in a rat-infested apartment surrounded by cops who wanted to kill them.

It was Maria who suggested after a romantic dinner and

a movie that they return to her small apartment. And it was Maria who made the first move and offered herself. They both took their time discovering the wonders of sex between lovers. They also found that they were both virgins, so their conversation during lovemaking was as much about pleasure as logistics. Her bed was small; often a leg or legs dangled over the edge of the narrow mattress. By early morning, the amateurs had managed to achieve their intimate goals and pleasures and had fallen deeply in love.

Maria asked as she ran a thin finger down his chest, "Are you going back to Rome at the end of the term?"

"My parents expect it, but this morning I'm not sure," Lucca countered.

"Good answer," she said, and gently bit his ear. "I've never been to Italy. Maybe we could go together. After all, you have met my parents. Maybe I should meet yours."

"That would be nice."

Then he remembered why he was in Chicago.

"But I do have to finish the term and some other duties," he added.

Maria hadn't asked any more questions beyond their earlier conversation. Now she didn't hide her annoyance.

"Is it something to do with those two so-called friends of yours? Lucca, you have to stop seeing them—they're trouble. I know kids like that and nothing good ever comes from being around them."

"It's something bigger than that. That's all I can say. Only when it's over, can I think of Italy and home. Until then, I'm trapped."

She rolled out of bed and took the top sheet with her. She draped the cloth around her shoulders, covering her breasts.

"You are never trapped unless it's a trap you make yourself," she told him.

She walked across the room, opened a dresser drawer and

took out a package of cigarettes.

"I didn't know you smoked."

"Only when I'm confused and annoyed. And, at the moment, I'm both in love with you and very exasperated."

She lit a cigarette and inhaled, exhaled. A trail of smoke billowed to the ceiling.

"You know what you need to do and won't," she said. "I don't want to know what you are involved with, but with those two it can't be good. All I can do is ask you to stop—stop for me."

"I can't."

"Or won't?"

She pulled another drawer open and began to pull out undergarments.

"I need to get to work," she said, her voice tight.

After she went into the small bathroom, Lucca sat on the edge of the bed, his head feeling as if it were spinning a hundred miles an hour. Maria had only told him what he already knew he needed to do, but with Sal, he knew it would not be easy.

"Strange thing, the other day," Maria said from the bathroom. "A woman came into the exhibit hall and asked for directions. She was very well dressed and quite a good-looking Italian. Tall and lanky. Her last name was Delucca, almost like your first name, so of course I remembered it. She also scared the hell out of me."

Lucca poked his head around the corner of the bathroom. "Why?"

"Don't you look in here, Lucca Barone. Can't a woman have a little privacy?"

"Why did she scare you?"

He backed away from the doorway and lit a cigarette.

"I don't know. It was just . . . odd. She touched my cheek, and it was like ice and fire at the same time. And with it came a quick smile that reminded me of a lioness I saw at the zoo, like a predatory leer. Anyway, it was probably nothing."

"Did you see her again?"

"No, I had other duties, and she left by another entry, I suspect. Now get out of here. I need to dress and so do you. We'll get some breakfast, then you need to get to school and me to work. Go, go."

Lucca dressed and watched as Maria put on her peasant's costume.

"You do look very cute," he said.

"When it was so hot, this was like being a wrapped chicken in an oven. Thankfully, at least the weather is more comfortable today. Even with those new-fangled air coolers, the pavilion can get hot."

After he had helped Maria climb onboard the bus that would take her to the fair, Lucca headed back to his foul-smelling apartment. He thought about the strange woman Maria mentioned. He was sure it was nothing, but it nagged at him. How could someone be that instantly terrifying?

17

ALFANO stayed at the Bridgeport street party long enough to watch the fireworks, then drove home and climbed the steps to his apartment. A paper bag with a bottle of, what he hoped was, Canadian Club whiskey in his hand. The landlord had replaced the bullet-shattered window at the landing (after making Alfano pay for it). The blood-soaked fake oriental carpet was now in some landfill, and the holes in the plaster wall had been patched and painted. It looked as if nothing had happened. Alfano knew better. As he turned at the landing, the door to the Kowalski's residence opened, and Alice Kowalski stood framed in the bright light of her apartment. A radio played in the background. Her right arm was still in a sling to help her broken shoulder heal faster.

"Late night, Detective?" Alice asked.

"Very late. Back from your vacation? How's the shoulder?"

"Yes, we came back this morning. It still hurts to high heaven, but each day is better. You want to come in for coffee? And we had a lovely time, even a little sunburn."

In the months before the shooting, Alice Kowalski had tried everything to seduce Tony into coming into her apartment while her husband was at work. She was of obvious Polish decent, with an ample figure and more-than-willing attitude, but Alfano drew the line at married women. Women like Alice were lonely, troubled and in desperate need of intimacy, something their husbands couldn't give after working twelve-hour shifts at the steel mill. In Alice Kowalski's case, the shooting proved to be a boon or, at least, a temporary reprieve from the monotony. Afterward, during her recovery, she and her husband had become much closer.

"Alice, I'm exhausted, and I have an early day tomorrow, but I appreciate the offer. Maybe later?"

"Always—the door is always open."

He felt this was now offered as a friendly request, rather than to an evening of questionable intimacies.

"Thanks. Good night, Alice."

"Good night, Detective. Have a nice holiday."

She smiled and slowly closed her apartment door.

Alfano placed the paper bag on the kitchen counter, rinsed a glass out from the sink and poured himself a drink. He wasn't a one-kind-of-liquor man; the years of Prohibition had turned him into an opportunist. He would drink whatever was available: Scotch, Canadian, Irish, even some very bad moonshine had passed his lips. Some he'd regretted, others surprised him, often because what he tasted was possibly the same thing as on the label.

The ringing of the phone, as if a fire engine was racing through the small bedroom, woke him sometime later.

"What? . . . Where? . . . You think it's the same killer? . . . Okay. I'll be there in an hour, Sergeant. . . . Yeah, I'm fine, actually damn good, except for your fucking call."

Forty-five minutes later, Alfano arrived at the station. The sun, just peeking over the low warehouse buildings to the east, added a blood-red glow to the sky.

Red sky at night, sailors' delight. Red skies at morning, sailors take warning.

"Why do you think it's the same killer," Alfano asked Mc-

Dunnah, as the sergeant placed a much-needed mug of coffee on the detective's desk.

"A woman was found in a flop in the Fifth District. We've been flagged across the city—when any of these killings happen, we are to be kept in the loop. That due to your keen and enduring friendship with His Honor."

Alfano gave his sergeant an impatient look.

"Get on with it."

McDunnah gave the address and the status of the victim: "a young black girl, strangled to death. According to the coroner, she'd been abused physically and sexually. She was found tied to the bed, a gag in her mouth."

"No fascist flag hidden somewhere?"

"No, or at least not one that was obvious to the coroner."

"Front desk?" Alfano asked.

"The old man at the flop's desk, a Chinaman, said that the girl had been to his place before, actually often. But her friends always came in through the back door. He never saw them."

"Convenient, and obviously could be anyone then."

"He also said, 'Late night, woman come down stair, all quick. Out door fast, no see face.' So maybe the John was a Jane?"

"Why? Do you think it's connected?"

"The victim was strangled with a length of silk rope identical to the ones we found at Bova's and the one you saw in Wisconsin. The boys are dropping it off later so we can compare the pieces. But it does sound similar."

"Any idea as to the victim?"

"One of the patrolmen on the scene knew the girl from some drug and prostitution arrests. She was called Minna Saint-John, originally from New Orleans. Came north with a piano player. She's been up here for maybe two years."

McDunnah looked at his notes.

"Her age was about twenty-two."

"Did he know where she worked, who her pimp was?"

"No pimp that he knew of," McDunnah said. But she worked at a club called Toutou's on Thirty-fifth. You know it?"

"Not as well as others in the district. It's fairly new, maybe four years old. Run by a serious bitch of a woman. Calls herself Madame Marie d'Pompadour. She'd sell her daughter for a hundred bucks. And it's a queer bar, but for women. Claims to be all French-like, but caters to a high-end all-girl crowd. It sounds like our killer has now moved on to include recreational killing in her repertoire."

Later that afternoon, Alfano held his star up to the bouncer at the entry to Toutou's.

"She in?" he asked the bouncer.

"Who wants to know?"

"Just tell her that Detective Alfano wants a few words. It's about Minna."

"What's she done now?" the bouncer said. "Madame Marie said if she git herself in trouble one more time, she can just rot in jail. She's all tired from bailing that skinny little bitch out."

"No bail required this time. Where's Madame Marie?"

The bouncer, his shoulders so broad, almost had to turn sideways to pass through the doorway. Spotlights set above the small corner stage cast silhouettes on the wall as Alfano followed him into the club. The jangling of a piano drifted in and out, in loose tempo with the eerie tones of a clarinet. The two men crossed the floor and wove their way through a jumble of tables and chairs; each small table was adorned with a half-melted candle in a raffia-wrapped wine bottle. The bouncer stopped at the end of the bar and whispered to a large black woman. Her beaded gown was cut low, barely covering her massive breasts that rose and fell with each puff she took from a cigarette stuck in an ebony holder.

She eyed Alfano, then said something to the bouncer, who took a last look at the detective before turning and leaving.

"A pleasure, I'm sure," the woman said to Alfano, not rising from her seat.

To his surprise, Madame Marie d'Pampadour's voice was like that of a fourteen-year-old, high-pitched and tight, as she held her hand out and introduced herself. Each of her thick fingers sported a gaudy ring.

"What can I do for you, Detective?"

ACERBI sat in her car across the street from Toutou's, having returned to watch for any signs of the police either coming or going. When a man exited a large black sedan and started talking to the bouncer, she was positive he was a cop. When he flashed his badge, all she did was smile. Distinguished was her first thought, and there was a tough look about him as well. Maybe Latin or even Italian; she settled on the latter. The cop stayed in the club for about fifteen minutes, then came out and lit a cigarette. Standing on the sidewalk, he jotted something in a notebook, smashed out his cigarette, and quickly left.

Madame d'Pompadour would pay for that carelessness, Acerbi promised silently.

The girl had been a trifle, a bit of fun, nothing more. As a child, Acerbi seldom had had toys or playthings, or even playmates. She'd always been bigger than most of the girls as well as the boys her age. Some had made fun of her size; after she found ways to hurt them, they stopped. By her fourteenth birthday, she had very few friends, and everyone else left her alone. Even then she'd known her place, her part in the world. Now when given an official order, she followed it unreservedly. Her commandant cared little for how Acerbi accomplished the orders, just that they were thoroughly completed.

However, finding these men was proving to be more difficult than expected. It had taken some further pressuring, but the weasel Barbieri was putting together a list of surnames to compare with the names and addresses she'd acquired from the college. Her plan then would be simple: to drive by each of the addresses and narrow the list. Matteo Bova hadn't been a complete waste, since she realized that seeing where each man lived would be a quick way to determine whether he was a recent arrival from Italy. The Bova residence had been too nice and lived-in for a student newly arrived in this country.

She tapped a finger on the steering wheel, feeling both impatient and eager. With only a week remaining to accomplish her orders, Acerbi needed to get back to work.

18

AFTER FUMBLING for the light switch on his bedside lamp, Alfano looked at his alarm clock. It was 5:38 a.m. The phone was ringing.

"Who's this?" he snapped into the mouthpiece. "Better be damned important.

It was important enough that he listened for three and one-half minutes, then slipped on his suit pants, brushed his teeth, washed his face, and combed out his thick hair. He unfolded a clean shirt from his dresser, found the dark tie with stripes that Gini had given him less than a month ago, and brushed the dust off his new shoes. Fully dressed, he walked out the door and down the stairs to the Packard. The morning sun cut through the overhead canopy of elms. The neighborhood traffic was light; maybe Chicagoans had slept in that morning. McDunnah was waiting for him outside the station.

"Sergeant," Alfano said, as he accepted a paper cup from McDunnah. "Where did they find this one?"

"A basement, on Giles near 37th."

"You drive," Alfano said, and slid over to the passenger side.

McDunnah pulled onto South Halsted and headed south.

"The message was waiting when I arrived, and since the

mayor is honoring you with this whole case, the other districts have been alerted," he told Alfano. "When they find a strangulation, call Alfano at Racine."

"I feel so blessed."

Alfano took a long sip of his now lukewarm coffee.

"How is it?"

Alfano took another sip.

"The coffee is like stale battery acid, but it's the thought that counts."

McDunnah shrugged. He'd worked with Anthony Alfano for almost ten years, the first few as a beat cop, then sergeant, and during that time he'd given up trying to turn Alfano into a morning person. A detective's job was cold nights and thick, wet heat, gift-wrapped around the hurt and the dead.

McDunnah was a third-generation cop. His grandfather Adam from County Cork, Ireland, had come to America just before the start of the Civil War. He and his younger brother had been sent off by their mother simply because she was too poor to take care of them. Adam joined the Union Army during the last year of the war and was mustered out without ever firing a shot. After the war, he was released from duty at a railroad station in Chicago with only his uniform and twenty dollars. Across the street was a police station, and he'd applied that day. He'd been a distinguished cop for thirty years. He'd married a bright girl from Bridgeport, where they raised three children, two boys, and a girl. McDunnah's father, Shamus, had been the eldest son and followed his father's profession and joined the Chicago force. During his twenty-second year on the job, Shamus, then a sergeant, took a slug in the leg from an Irish gangster during a bank robbery. The damage was so bad they had to cut the left leg off above the knee; now ten years later, he owned a bar in Bridgeport. Sergeant McDunnah was the older of Shamus's two boys; the younger brother had died during the influenza outbreak in 1917. That same year,

McDunnah's grandfather Adam died from the same rapacious disease. McDunnah had joined the force in 1914 and had been Alfano's sergeant at Racine since 1929. He admired Alfano and had more respect for the detective than any other cop he knew on the force. His only disappointment was that Anthony Alfano was an absolute bastard most mornings—and today was just one more.

"You still going to the game this afternoon?" he asked Alfano, as they drove the quiet early morning streets.

"Depends on what we find this morning."

"It's an order by His Honor; he'd be sorely disappointed if you didn't show, I think."

"I don't give a rat's ass about that political hack. And you?"

"I would also be very disappointed, Detective. We don't get out much. It might be good for our souls. Besides, this may be the last time we see the Bambino. He's getting up there in years."

"Sergeant, you are one year older than that left-fielding Yankee son of a bitch. The way he messes around off the field, I wouldn't be surprised if he dropped dead before he's fifty."

"Yankee or not, he's one for the ages."

Alfano stared out the window.

"Yes, he's definitely that. One for the ages."

Two prowlers sat outside the two-story brick house; the coroner's van and two official-looking sedans were double parked on the street. Nine wooden steps led up to the covered porch of the well-tended clapboard home. Behind and below the porch, Alfano saw another door that opened into what he assumed was a half-basement. A patrolman stood at the top of the steps that led down to the basement door. Three other men stood on the sidewalk one house down. One was a photographer, the other two obviously reporters. Across the street, a small cluster of black neighbors stood, impatiently watching.

Alfano and McDunnah gave their names to the patrolman

on the steps and then proceeded into the basement. The small room, more like a basement studio, was crammed with cops. The thick aroma of death hung in the rising heat, a product of the humid morning, a dozen sweating men, and a body.

"They called you—good," said the coroner. "When I saw the victim, I immediately thought of you."

"Not sure I appreciate the acknowledgment," Alfano replied. "Why?"

"This is why."

The coroner elbowed aside two of the police officers to open a corridor to another room in the rear. There a uniformed cop and a detective stood, looking at the body of a woman bound upright on a wooden chair. She was very large, very black, and obviously dead. Her arms were tied to the chair arms. One leg of the chair had broken off but remained tied to the woman's left leg. Why she hadn't tumbled over was a mystery. A length of white rope was still fastened around her neck. Her tongue protruded and her eyes were flushed with red. And she was nude.

"Good God," McDunnah said softly.

"Obviously, God wasn't there to stop them," Alfano said. "How long?"

"Rigor is still set. That's why she's not fallen over," the coroner explained. "Her leg is acting as the fourth leg of the chair. There's significant lacerations to both wrists and ankles. My deduction is that as she was strangled, she broke the chair's leg away. Not too many men could do that, I'll tell you that. I'll know more when I complete the autopsy."

Alfano walked slowly around the body, looking carefully at both the damage and the woman.

"Is it necessary to leave her naked like that?" McDunnah said. "For Christ's sake, can't we have some decency? Someone get a sheet or a blanket."

"Well, she's not one of your Irish lasses," one of the local district cops said.

Alfano looked hard at the cop.

"You keep your fucking mouth shut. One more remark like that, and I'll kick your bony Polish ass out the fucking door. Dr. Abrahamson, could you place a sheet over the lady?"

"Yes, sir. Be right back."

Alfano examined the woman even more closely. The cop with the smart mouth started to say something. Alfano just looked at the man until he stopped and muttered something about checking upstairs, then left.

"Well, that cleared the air," McDunnah said.

"Notice anything different here than the others, Sergeant?" Alfano asked.

McDunnah studied the body and rope marks.

"Her hands, they're not damaged. Not busted up like the others," he said. "So you think that this might not be our killer?"

"Fairly certain it was. The rope is very similar, but this murder was different. There isn't torture to find something out; this was a premeditated act of punishment. There's some bite marks here and here."

McDunnah and the other detective looked where Alfano pointed. It was hard to see the marks on the chocolate-brown skin.

"Damn, that's just weird," the local detective said.

The coroner returned with a sheet, which he draped over the body.

"Did you get your photos, Doctor?"

"I got them, Tony. That's the first thing I did. In this heat, I need to document as much as I can before we move her. If the woman who lives upstairs hadn't come home early from a holiday in Gary, the only way anyone would have found her was through the odor of decay."

"Pleasant thought," Alfano said.

Now with the cloth draped over the body, only the head was visible. Its temporary if bizarre separation from the rest of the body changed both the appearance of the face and the grotesque nature of the murder.

"Damn, I know this woman," Alfano said. "Let me think. I got it here."

He retrieved one of the small notebooks from his suit pocket and flipped through the pages.

"Madame Marie d'Pompadour."

"You're kidding, right?" McDunnah said.

"No, she owned the lesbian bar where Minna Saint-John worked. Seems that Madame Marie made one too many enemies."

ACERBI parked a block from the Southside tenement where several police cars and a coroner's van sat. She watched with interest as each person went in and out of the basement apartment, smiled when one of the cops retched into the flowerbed just outside the stairway.

That will teach that bitch to talk to the police.

She was surprised how quickly they'd discovered the body; maybe it was the woman from upstairs. Acerbi had covered her tracks, they would find nothing at the scene, but what she was really doing was teasing the cops. When the Italian detective showed, she knew she'd caught the mouse. This cop was someone to watch, and it occurred to her that maybe, just maybe, he'd be able to help her find the three men she was looking for. All she needed was a bigger piece of cheese to fully get his attention.

19

FOR MONTHS it had been difficult for anyone in Chicago to avoid news of the forthcoming expedition of Mussolini's second-in-command, Air Marshall Italo Balbo. Everyone knew that Balbo was flying from Italy to Chicago with his squadron of twenty-four Savoia-Marchetti S-55 seaplanes to celebrate the Century of Progress World's Fair. Each day, on some page of the *Tribune*, there was a report of the preparation and progress of the adventure. Sketches and the occasional photographic headshot of the aviator and his past travels and triumphs in Brazil teased the readers. Chicago's large Italian community was ecstatic over the possibilities the summer held for their home country as well as their new home on the shores of Lake Michigan.

Every young Italian boy in the city had memorized the route of the international adventure. Balbo and his squadron would leave Orbetello (about 75 miles north of Rome) on July 1st to fly to Amsterdam. From there they would fly to Northern Ireland, then Iceland, and then the New World with the first stop being in Labrador, then New Brunswick. If all went well, they would arrive in Chicago from Montreal in a total of eight days. Each leg of the journey allowed enough safe leeway for the airplane's 1,850-mile range. The newspapers cautioned that, even in summer, the squadron might be delayed due to weather as it crossed the North Atlantic. Celebrations in Chicago were scheduled so as to be flexible since the exact arrival time of the guest of honor was anyone's guess. By the afternoon of the All-Star baseball game, Balbo and his crews were stranded in Iceland. When they could leave, no one was sure.

For many aviation aficionados, the Savoia-Marchetti was the greatest airplane flying. Originally designed as a torpedo bomber after the Great War, its twin hulls supported a central flight deck that held the pilot and crew of the flying boat. The two hulls were used to carry cargo and passengers. Overhead, two inline counter-rotating propellers literally pushed and pulled the airplane with twin engines mounted back to back, each engine exerting over eight hundred horsepower. For six years the aircraft had set records for speed, altitude and distance. It had earned fame with crossings of the Atlantic between Western Europe and Brazil and Argentina. Many of these flights had preceded Charles Lindbergh's historic solo crossing of the Atlantic. The Italians had always thought the Americans were late to the game.

Before leaving Rome, Sal Rizzo had spent an afternoon in a café with his political mentor, who tutored the young man about the airplane and its operation.

"While formidable, they have a weakness," the communist professor said. "They are made of wood, like a child's plaything. Thin layers of plywood are secured to frames and struts made of spruce and ash. They burn like a fascist bonfire when they crash."

"So?"

"Don't be dense, my boy. All you have to do is set them on fire. There's no need for bombs or trying to acquire other, more difficult explosives. All you need to do is douse them with petrol, throw a match, then run."

"They are seaplanes, comrade. It will be hard to run on the water."

"True, but I am sure you will find a way."

Sal had spent two months thinking about how to douse the planes. One afternoon, he carried a small jar of gasoline and a wooden model boat to an out-of-the-way inlet on Lake Michigan. He poured the gasoline on the surface of the water, lit a match and set fire to a handful of newspapers. He touched the flame to the fumes rising from the gasoline. In seconds the model boat caught fire; he knew then what needed to be done.

He explained the operation to his two associates—to call them friends was inappropriate. They were functionaries, nothing more. After the planes were burned, he would quickly leave and head back to Italy via Miami, alone. Lucca and Matteo would be on their own. Sal's plan reduced the chance of his being caught and, with the other two presumably still in Chicago, increased theirs.

Twice Sal and Matteo walked the small inlet in Lincoln Park to agree on the best boat for their operation. If anything, they wanted to be certain that when they needed the boat it would be there. This time when they arrived, the cruiser with *Blackhawk* painted on its stern was still anchored to its buoy.

"She hasn't moved," Sal said. "I think that she will do."

Matteo nodded.

"One week, that's my guess," Sal continued. "That pompous fascist Balbo should be here by the twelfth of July, or not much later."

They had the gasoline and flare guns. All they needed was good weather and a distraction, he said to Matteo, restating what they both knew.

"They say there will be a parade," Matteo replied.

"Good for us—everybody will be watching that."

"I can hot-wire the motor," Matteo said, looking back at the boat. "After the operation, we can tie her up anywhere. I hope she's fast enough to make our escape."

"I'm sure of it."

But Matteo wasn't sure. In fact after almost three months

in America, he wasn't sure about a lot of things he'd been sure of back in Rome. What he was absolutely positive about was that there was no way he would allow himself to be caught after the attack. If he had to, under the cover of night, he would point the boat north and disappear in either of the states to the north, Michigan or Wisconsin. He had to admit, though, that he was vague as to how to set a course or how big Lake Michigan truly was. More than once he'd told himself to just follow Sal's directions and remember his comforting words: 'I'll keep you safe, Matteo. Trust me.' Even though Sal was making it easier, after all this time, he still wasn't sure whether to follow or try to lead.

Both men had written off Lucca Barone. After he'd fallen for Maria, all Sal could say was, "He has a dick for a brain. One sweet look and he's worthless. Maybe I should just shoot the son of a bitch and be done with it. If there's a problem, it could come from him or more likely her. Maybe shoot them both."

"You wouldn't do that," Matteo said.

"If this get's fucked up, I will shoot that love-struck asshole. Till then, we tell him as little as possible, *capisce?*"

"*Capisce.*"

"TWO BEERS, AL," McDunnah said to the bartender. "We're here to celebrate our American League boys and their glorious four-to-two victory over the lads of the National League. That game was something! Nothing like it."

"I held your table in the back, Sergeant," came the affable answer.

Alfano looked at McDunnah.

"I've known you for more than ten years and this is the first time you've invited me to your private club."

"Detective, don't you know drinking is illegal in these here

United States? This is a private Irish social club, and we are quite particular about our patrons."

McDunnah reached across the bar and took the two large glass steins the bartender had set out; then he and Alfano elbowed their way through the thick tangle of Irishmen to a small booth in the rear. A large *Reserved* card was propped up against a jar of pickled eggs on the table top.

"Nice, very nice," Alfano said.

"Nice? Hell, this is one of the best clubs here in Bridgeport. The waiting list is years long unless you know someone."

McDunnah raised his beer glass.

"*Sláinte!*"

"Your health!"

A large man came up to their booth and slapped McDunnah on the back.

"You ever seen a game like that, Mac? I mean ever," the big man said. "By the Holy Martyrs, nothing like it. The Babe, Al Simmons, Gehrig . . ."

"Don't forget the Nationals"—McDunnah ticked off names with the fingers of his left hand—"Pepper Martin, Chuck Klein, Frankie Frisch and Hallahan."

McDunnah introduced his friend, Terrance O'Flaterey: "Terry to his friends," the sergeant told Alfano.

O'Flaterey reached across the table and shook Alfano's hand with his huge paw. A small taste of suds hung to the corner of the man's thick red beard.

"Pleasure, Detective. Mac has told me a lot about ya. Good to meet ya."

"The honor's mine, Terry."

"He works for the ballpark," McDunnah told Alfano. "No one loves baseball more than Terry."

The big man nodded.

"I've seen the Babe hit a lot of homers in that ballpark over the years," he said. "But this one today was special."

He closed his eyes as if re-seeing the two-run shot to drive in Gehringer, then the glorious catch made by Ruth in the eighth inning to steal a homer from Chick Hafey.

"We may never see another game with all these greats on the same field," Terry told them. "Yes, sir, maybe never."

"Forty-nine thousand people may change reluctant minds. My guess, this isn't the last time they'll play it. Where there's money to be made, who knows," McDunnah said.

"Always the cynic, Sergeant," Alfano added.

"I'd be playing second fiddle to your attitude, Detective. Some mornings—never seen anyone so dour." McDunnah said, and raised his mug.

"Terry, what's the word on Al Simmons?" Alfano asked, wisely changing the subject.

"We got him for a song. Ol' Connie Mack didn't know what to do with him. So he sold him to the Sox, best deal of the century. Now he has a chance to win the MVP. What the hell is better than that? From my seat with the other lads out beyond the bullpen, we saw a great game."

"Can you believe those Saint Louis boys had four men on the team?" another Irishman piped up as he passed McDunnah's booth.

"They be the enemy, Mickey," Terry said. "The enemy, I tell you. The Cubs will never win a pennant as long as those Cardinals are there."

"The Cubs? Terry, where's your loyalty?" McDunnah asked.

"With Comiskey and my Sox, Mac. But my heart goes out to those poor boys in blue on the North Side."

"Send them a card."

A waif of an Irish girl sidled up and slid her arm under Terry's left arm. She smiled up at the man.

"A beer, Terry, love. Please."

"Just a sec, Annie," O'Flaterey said to the redhead, her skin as white as a winter's full moon. "I be a'talken."

"Terry . . ."

"Gents, got to go. The missus is pulling my chain. Please, Detective, anytime you need a ticket let me know. I know's people."

He put his finger against his nose and winked.

"Seems like a good fellow," Alfano said to McDunnah.

"He is. We grew up together. A little trouble when he was young—he had a tough family life. All the usual problems of an alcoholic father, sick mother, five siblings and no work. He was lucky to get the Comiskey Park job. It helped to settle him. Old Charles Comiskey personally gave him the job, both of their families being from Crosserlough. Lately, with all the troubles in Ireland, there's a few rumors about Terry's involvement with some local Irish groups. I've told him to be cautious."

"He should be very careful, as we've found during the last fifteen years," answered Alfano, referring to the number of 'bad lads' who'd come to America to escape the British and then hung around, causing mischief."

"Don't I know it."

"Thanks for the tour and the beer, Sergeant. I'm going home. This is my first day off in two weeks, and I intend to enjoy what's left of it. It has been a very mean and nasty business these past weeks, and I fear we're not a step closer to finding this killer."

Alfano started to slide out of the booth.

"I've been thinking, maybe there's another reason for this," McDunnah said. "From what Dr. Abrahamson is telling us, this is one very seriously fucked-up killer. She, if we're right about the sex, goes for girls and is not nice about it. Now this Madame Marie killing—way over the top, sadistic."

Alfano halted his exit and reached for what remained of his beer.

"Beyond fucked up," he said. "There's nothing about these killings that shows even the slightest hint of remorse. That woman is after something."

"It *may* be a woman," cautioned McDunnah.

"I'm sure of it. Which makes it even harder to chase down. The description that Madame Marie gave matches the one we got from the cab driver. Remember Doolan said she had an accent, and d'Pompadour said that too. That Italian accent may be the connection to the DeAngelos and Bova, but the two women from the club, they may be a result of her other . . . interests."

"Okay, I'll give you the woman angle—for now. If we concentrate on the Italian angle, then we're fairly certain this is not related to the Outfit or the mob, at least no connections that I can see. And, two of the killings were more than a hundred miles away in Wisconsin, so it's not a purely local thing."

Alfano listened carefully. McDunnah wasn't saying anything they both didn't know, but the sergeant's deductive abilities were spot on, and this case had them both puzzled.

"The DeAngelos were immigrants from Italy; maybe this has something to do with where they came from," McDunnah continued. "Something they brought or maybe they were followed. The chief of police in Wisconsin did say the neighbors thought the DeAngelos had some sympathies with the communists."

"Unsubstantiated, but you make a point," Alfano said. "With all the craziness of Italian politics right now, there's really only two groups of importance in Italy, the fascists and the communists—and they do not play nice with each other."

"Paper, Sargent?" a kid said to McDunnah.

His head barely a foot higher than the top of the table, the ruddy, freckled face of the boy screamed Irish.

"Paper? Latest on the game and the fair."

"Sure, Foyle."

McDunnah slid a dime across the table.

"Keep it," he said.

"Thanks, Sarg. Best to the family."

Foyle handed over a paper from the bundle he carried under his arm and whirled back into the crowd.

"Americans win first All-Star game—Balbo in Iceland," they heard him yell as he disappeared into the mash of bodies.

Echoing the boy's cry, **BALBO IN ICELAND** in bold black type headlined the neWspaper.

"Quite something, don't you think, Sergeant?" Alfano said, tapping the headline. "It's a strange and wondrous time we're living in. To think that someone could be on one side of the world last week, then right here in Chicago the next is beyond my understanding. I know it's real and the world is changing fast, but still . . ."

"I understand. Not only people move about, but with them come their ideas, beliefs, culture, religion, and—"

"Hatreds?" Alfano interjected.

"Yeah, them too."

Alfano finished his beer and continued to stare at the paper. His eyes scanned down the copy under the headline.

"Sergeant, what's the most exciting thing happening right now?"

"That cute lass that's walking this way. Damn, I can't remember her name."

Alfano looked up and smiled.

"No, Sarg, I mean in the city."

McDunnah grinned ruefully as he looked back at Alfano, then at the paper.

"Damn, you're right. It's got to be Balbo and his flying boats. Every day the *Tribune* screams the latest about where they landed, who they met, even what they ate. Have to say, it's really caught the imagination of the people of Chicago. From what I've read, they're still not sure when they'll arrive. But the town's on pins and needles."

"Let me throw this at you: maybe someone doesn't want

Balbo to succeed."

"Succeed? Hell, he's just flying twenty-four airplanes here from Italy. It's so damn dangerous, there's a better-than-even chance some of them won't make it. So why bother?"

"It's two entirely different things; to crash and die is hardly the same as an assassination. One shows heroism, the other hatred. Suppose there's a faction that wants to embarrass the fascists here in the United States, here in Chicago?"

"How?" McDunnah wanted to know. "By shooting down the planes like ducks on the wing as they start to land on Lake Michigan?"

"That would be too difficult. No, I'm thinking after they land. They'd be sitting ducks, to use your image. Whoever is behind this would want to somehow damage or destroy the planes and disgrace the fascists, show them that they are vulnerable anywhere."

"The communists?"

"Best guess—yeah."

"You think this woman is working for the communists and is waiting for Balbo?"

"No, I think she's working for the fascists and is trying to stop this from happening. We need to be looking for more than this bitch; we need to be looking for someone who's trying to fuck Mussolini."

20

GUIDO BARBIERI slid a full-size envelope across the table to Acerbi.

"My people have narrowed down the choices to these. They all have connections to the Sapienza Rome University, and my people there tell me one of the professors is well known as a communist sympathizer. All three were in his classes."

"I thought all the Bolsheviks were purged from the universities," Acerbi answered.

"Some are less demonstrative. They have given us no reason . . . yet."

Acerbi opened the envelope. Inside were three folders; each had a name printed on the front. She opened the one labeled *Matteo Cavallo* and immediately looked at the small passport photo clipped to the first page, then read through the five paragraphs. She briefly looked at the contents of the other folders.

"He looked nothing like this one," she said, putting her finger on the grainy image of Cavallo.

"Who?"

Acerbi started to answer, then stopped; Matteo Bova was hardly a thought now.

"Are these addresses correct?" she asked Barbieri.

"How should I know? They are what the consulate has posted, so I assume they are. It will be your job to confirm them."

"If they are not correct, if I waste one more day—I will make very sure that Rome knows."

"Do not threaten me. I want these men stopped as much as you do. We have come so far with the fair and all that we have done here. They could cause immeasurable harm to the cause and our reputations if they get to Balbo."

"Then good-bye. If I'm successful, you will not hear from me again. If I fail, and it's due to some involvement by anyone at the embassy or the fair, I assure you, you will see me again."

Acerbi left through the rear service door, which offered a temporary reprieve from the crowds that filled the promenades and walkways connecting the fair pavilions. The heavy, humid air was made thicker by cigar and cigarette smoke. The drone of a hundred-thousand voices seemed to suck up any breathable air that was left. Across the North Lagoon, people sat on the promenade steps with their feet dangling in the cool waters of Lake Michigan. Acerbi exited the fairgrounds via the entry between the Field Museum and the Shedd Aquarium and took a taxi to the corner of North LaSalle and Schiller. She would walk the rest of the way to her apartment. So doing would give her a chance to see if she was being followed.

At a diner on North Boulevard, she took a back booth and watched the door. If the FBI or some other cop were following her, this is where she'd spot them. After twenty minutes, no one suspicious had entered. She looked more carefully through the three folders. Lucca Barone, Salvatore Rizzo, and Matteo Cavallo: there was nothing peculiar or remarkable about any of them, although the softness to Barone's eyes intrigued her. Nothing about Rizzo surprised her; he had a callous look and probably was. She guessed him to be the leader. Cavallo looked stout, and with his pugilist's nose, was probably the muscle.

She decided to focus on him; maybe without the group's *muscolo*, the threesome would be easier to stop.

The same address appeared on the immigration forms for all three, in the 2700 block of North Wilton. Later, in the cool of the evening, she drove slowly by the house to check the address and waited an hour to see what might happen. Other than some pedestrians out strolling in the comfortable evening, no one showed. This time she would make sure that this Matteo was the right Matteo.

The address was a modest, single-story clapboard house with a porch extended across the front. Ten wooden steps climbed up from the sidewalk. A screen door partially hid the front door behind a gray haze of woven wire. A short hedge of yews masked the base of the porch. Some hostas, their leaves shredded by slugs, poked out from under the skirt of the yews. The house and the whole of the street were shaded by great sycamores that lined both sides of the approach.

The next morning Acerbi parked halfway up the block for two hours and then returned for another three hours in the afternoon. Still no one arrived or left the house. The shade of the sycamores made the stakeout endurable. Every five minutes the rumble and clatter of the elevated train that ran above the backyards of the houses on Milford shattered the quiet. She could not understand how anyone could live with that contraption not fifty feet above their rear windows. Maybe a person could get used to anything if the rent was right.

Late in the afternoon of the first day, a gang of kids surrounded her car and asked what she was doing on their street. She gave them an answer about police, a stakeout, and bad guys that seemed to impress them. She swore them to secrecy. They didn't bother her again that afternoon, but she watched them in the car's mirrors as they watched her. In the last hour of the second day, two men purposely approached from up the street, stopped in front of the house and lit cigarettes. She knew their faces. Five minutes later, they went inside.

"Those dagos friends of yours?" a voice asked just outside her open window.

Startled, Acerbi jerked her head to the left and looked into the face of a boy about nine years old. He was one of the members of the posse she'd talked to the day before.

"Dagos?" she asked.

"Yeah, dagos, wops, eye-ties, greaseballs."

"You mean Italian?"

"Sure, my friend Mario's a dago."

The child pointed toward the five kids that held back about thirty feet.

"He says those guys are the real thing all the way from Italy."

"You talk to them?"

The kid stared at Acerbi.

"You're pretty, but you got an accent. Why do you want to know? You a dago?"

"Just wondering. Have you talked to them?"

"Maybe a month or so back, they was waiting at the corner for a cab. I asked them, real friendly like if there was anything us boys could do to help them, for a quarter, you know."

"And?"

"They told us to get lost. Mario said that was no way to talk to a fellow Italian. The big guy took Mario by the shoulder and told him to get lost. Mario said, 'Fuck you.' That's when we all ran. Still laugh about it."

"Tough guys."

"Yeah, we're real tough. You have to be these days. Are they your friends?"

"No, I'm just observing them. They are part of an important case. So you won't say anything; can I have your word and the word of your gang?"

"We're not a gang, we are a club. And yes, we won't say

nothing. You sound like a dago though. You eye-talian?"

"Yes, my family came from Italy many years ago. Now I do private investigations."

"A private dick? Too cool. Never met a woman P.I."

"What do you know about detectives and gangsters?"

"I go to hundreds of movies, all of us do. Edward G. Robinson, George Raft, Cagney, tough guys," the boy said, as if proud of his knowledge.

"So, you know what happens when you don't keep a secret?" she said, her voice turning cold."

The kid paused, about to say something, then the real meaning behind her remark sank in. He hung his head a bit, then said, "Yeah, sure. Gotta go." He quick-walked back to his buddies.

She watched the boys in the rearview mirror and smiled to herself.

Dagos, wops, guineas. In a short time, the world will fear us. Then we shall see what they call us.

21

ALFANO slowly closed the door to his apartment, heard the lock set, and headed down the stairs. His goal: to escape being apprehended by Alice Kowalski on the landing. Even though it was early, the noise from the unit directly under his meant one thing—the Kowalskis were up. That wasn't unusual; Mr. Kowalski would often leave early to catch the trolley to the steel plant. What concerned Tony was Alice's loud and demanding voice. Not a good sign.

He'd made it three steps past the landing when the Kowalski door opened—not really opened, more like blown out by the big hands of Mr. Kowalski. The exterior wall received the full impact of the door handle, leaving a deep dent in the lath and plaster. Kowalski, easily fifty pounds heavier and four inches taller than Alfano, glared at the detective. Swinging his lunch pail as if trying to clear a path ahead of himself, he stomped passed Alfano and down the steps toward the glass door of the entry foyer. Alfano feared for the glass. The words he heard Mr. Kowalski mutter under his breath sounded Polish, with a few phrases in English, including 'stupid cow,' mixed in with the Slavic phrasing.

Alfano remained on the step, wishing to flee but also knowing it was too late.

"That son of a bitch," came Alice's voice through the open door. "He thinks I'm fooling around behind his back. Me, a good Catholic girl, well schooled by the Dominican sisters and brought up right. He's a suspicious son of a bitch."

She stepped out onto the landing and stood too close to him.

"Tony, have I ever done anything that would make you think I was that kind of woman?"

Alfano hadn't a clue as to how to answer her question. His first thought was, which time? For all he knew, she never fooled around. Maybe she was one of those tease artists he'd run into in speaks and clubs, maybe. Then again maybe she was a lonely woman who saw nothing at the end of the road except more road, or a cliff, or terminal boredom. Alfano wasn't sure he wanted to know. All he wanted that minute was to follow Mr. Kowalski down the stairs as fast as possible.

"You want some eggs, Detective?" she was saying. "His lordship didn't even finish his bacon, so's I have eggs, some fine bacon, and some toast. You interested?"

"Alice, that sounds great, but I can't," Alfano told her, even though he was actually very hungry. "I have to be at the station; the desk sergeant called and said something's up."

"I didn't hear no phone."

She put a hand over her mouth.

"You can hear my phone?"

"Sometimes," Alice said softly.

She looked regretful, as if realizing that she'd made a mistake by letting Alfano know how thin the walls and floors were.

"I got it just as it started to ring," he lied. "Got to go. Have a nice day."

Before she could answer, he was down the steps and out the foyer door; it clicked shut behind him. He made a beeline for his Packard, realizing that it was probably time to move. While he and Alice Kowalski had shared a very brutal and life-threatening moment less than a month earlier, it was becoming quite obvious that they could not live in the same apartment building.

"Anyone else dead today, Sergeant?" Alfano asked when he arrived at the station.

"I guess we were lucky. However, it is early," McDunnah replied, as the detective passed by the front counter and headed for his desk. "No new bodies. Every district is alerted, especially after our conversation earlier in the week, but nothing."

"I take it you didn't include our speculation in information sent out?"

"No, I thought it best to keep it to ourselves. We'd look pretty foolish if it turned out to be something else."

"Rock and a hard place," Alfano said. "I thought about it a lot and it makes sense from some crazy point of view. But to put the whole city on alert over this, not sure."

"By the way, the boys working the fair brought that in about an hour ago."

McDunnah pointed to a package on the table in the station's foyer.

"What do you think?" Alfano asked.

"It had been handed over to police this morning, they think that it might be a bomb. General Italo Balbo's name, in care of the Italian pavilion, is neatly printed on the label. The return address was in New Jersey.

"Everyone's so paranoid over all this Balbo stuff," Alfano answered. "Now we're suspicious of packages. And New Jersey communists? Hell, half the state's Italian. Open it, Sergeant."

"Not a chance. I'm waiting for the experts. They're supposed to be here anytime."

"We may not have time. What can happen?" Alfano asked.

"We could end up being the victims of a mad bomber out for revenge on the fascists and in a thousand bloody pieces spread all over this part of the city."

"I really don't care, Sergeant," Alfano said. "Look around. Nothing is getting done, and most of the people want to be somewhere else."

"Give it ten minutes, tops. Then we can look at the package and see what we can do."

It was the longest ten minutes Alfano ever remembered. He recalled the phone ringing and then McDunnah talking. He didn't remember why. Enough, he thought. Enough.

He'd been pacing and now walked purposefully to the table, reached into his pocket and retrieved his a long, folded pocketknife. To the shock of everyone in the station, Alfano opened the knife and slowly slid the blade along the seam of the outside brown paper. In short order, he'd removed the outer paper and stopped. No letter inside, no secret trip wire. He slowly raised the lid of the now exposed box. Inside was a cake.

"Do you think General Balbo would have a problem if we take a bite or two?" McDunnah asked a few seconds later, to the sounds of relieved laughter.

"You think it's safe? It might be poisoned. Only one way to find out," Alfano said.

He cut a narrow slice from the center outward and took a bite. Moments later, the cake disappeared into the mouths of the cops in the Racine Street station.

"We got lucky," Alfano said. "Next time, it might be a real bomb."

"Call city hall and try to get me a meeting with Kelly," he told the sergeant. "I think it would be prudent to offer the mayor a little taste of our paranoia."

Sergeant McDunnah headed to his phone, another piece of cake in his hand. Alfano scanned the murder board and noticed that the sergeant had pinned up some handbills from the Century of Progress Fair along with a picture of General

Italo Balbo, waving from the cockpit of one of his seaplanes. The news was that Balbo and his squadron were still stuck in Iceland and when they would reach Chicago was still—up in the air.

Two hours later, Alfano cooled his heels in the outer office of the mayor. He was uncomfortable. Even though he'd requested the meeting, he felt like he was waiting to see the school principal. Aside from his general dislike of the current mayor, he had never liked authority, especially elected authority. He preferred hierarchies and levels of command; responsibilities went up and down that chain of command. For years in this town, politicians—from the aldermen to the mayor—had given off an air of entitlement that stunk up city hall. Alfano always felt like checking his pockets when he left city hall meetings, just to make sure he still had the buck he'd had when he came in.

The black box on the secretary's desk buzzed.

"He will see you now," the dour woman said.

It was obvious she did not approve of Detective Anthony Alfano sticking his nose into her very busy schedule this morning.

"Detective, it is great to see you. Wasn't that ballgame fantastic?" the mayor said, before Alfano was halfway through the door. "Damn fine thing for the city. Did you know they are thinking of doing it every year? Now that's something, and we can say that it started here. My late predecessor, God rest his soul, was very instrumental in making it a part of the festivities for the fair. Maybe I can convince the baseball commissioner to have it here next year as well."

"We had a fine time, thank you," Alfano offered, when he was able to get a word in.

"And today the boys in Springfield will ratify the repeal of the Eighteenth Amendment," the mayor went on, as if Alfano hadn't spoken. "We'll be the tenth state. Patrick Nash is down there right now, making it happen."

Alfano had wondered where Kelly's puppet master was; thankfully, he wouldn't have to deal with both of them this morning.

"Your sergeant said you had something to tell me about these killings. He was a little circumspect—"

The mayor pointed to a chair, and Alfano sat down.

"It's just a theory, in fact, way out there, all things considered," Alfano said. "I want to follow it up, but it's important that you be in the loop."

"You are my top detective. I trust you implicitly. You have the interests of the city deep in your soul."

Alfano, at that moment, almost decided that the whole idea was preposterous and would only blow up in his face.

"It's only an idea, far out to be sure, but it's an idea as to what these killings are about," he said carefully.

"Go on, you have my attention and fifteen minutes before a group of Czechoslovakian visitors come storming in for some photos."

Alfano outlined his theory that the killings were part of a plan to undermine Balbo's convoy. As each minute passed, he could see that Mayor Kelly was becoming more and more agitated.

"Stop, Detective. Have you told anyone else, other than your sergeant, any of this?"

"No, sir. No one."

Kelly was now pacing about his office; he'd lit a cigar and was puffing like a runaway locomotive. Alfano was sure it was because Nash was not on hand. At the moment, Mayor Kelly had only himself as counsel and that was not serving him well. Alfano watched as the political animal emerged.

"That's good, very good. Tell no one. Do you understand, Detective? No one. If that damned McCormick and his fucking paper catch wind of this, I can tell you what will happen.

You can be damn sure when those twenty-four planes reach American shores, they will go straight to New York and not even think about coming any further west. It would be a disaster."

"I said it's only a theory, speculation."

"Speculation is what started the Depression, Alfano. I want facts—hard facts—and I want this speculation to be only between you and me. Outside of your sergeant, talk about this with no one else. When Nash gets back tonight, I'll go over it with him. You and I will talk in the morning. The word from the Italian consul is that Balbo will be leaving Iceland tomorrow on their way to Montreal. If this, and I mean if, is happening, you will have three days to stop it."

22

THE MORNING BALBO and his air fleet lifted off the Saint Lawrence River in Montreal heading to Chicago, Sal and Matteo pushed one of the small dinghies from the beach out into the lagoon. Not a soul could be seen on the small inlet's surrounding walks and pathways. Matteo slipped the oars into their locks and began to slowly row out toward the three-dozen motorboats and launches tied to buoys.

"The *Blackhawk* is still there, excellent," Sal said. "Row behind it and we will tie up on its backside."

"Port side," Matteo said. "Port is on the left."

"So what? I don't want anyone from shore to see us."

When they were close enough, Sal grabbed the rail of the launch and tied the dinghy to a cleat on the boat's gunnel. In a second, he was over the rail. He tossed a canvass bag on the deck and immediately looked around to make sure the boat was unoccupied. He removed a small crowbar from the bag and jimmied open the cruiser's main door and slipped inside. After a few seconds, he came out.

"Our luck is holding. No one is on board," he called up to Matteo.

Matteo didn't ask what Sal would have done if there had been people on board. The pistol stuck in Sal's waistband scared him.

"Please be empty," he had prayed with every stroke of the oars.

"You get the motor started. I'll check on the mooring lines and how much fuel. We'd be seriously fucked if we ran out of gasoline," Sal told him.

Matteo climbed the narrow stair that led to the bridge and the boat's controls. He looked at the console for a place to insert a key; there wasn't one.

"We may be lucky again," he yelled down to Sal. "She may start without a key. I won't have to hot-wire it."

"What are you waiting for? Give it a try," came the answer.

Matteo looked at the dashboard, full of small and large dials. One said RPM, another FUEL, and continuing across the mahogany panel were gauges for oil pressure, amps, and volts. Another panel held a column of switches for lights and fuses. To the right was a stainless throttle with a red knob. Above was the red starter button. His primary concern was for the fuel level, RPMs, and amps when he switched on the various electrical systems and batteries.

"Switching on the batteries," he yelled. "Don't pull the anchor until I start the motor."

He flipped the various switches, keeping an eye on the battery indicator as the gauges came to life.

"Battery is full, and so is the fuel tank," he reported.

"Excellent. Try the motor."

Matteo hit the starter button, and there came a rumbling from beneath the open rear deck. A blast of black smoke belched from the exhaust. Then the engine sputtered to a stop.

"What's the matter?" Sal demanded, as he came to Matteo's side.

"Patience. It's been a few years since I operated one of these."

Matteo located the choke and pulled the knob halfway,

tried the starter again, and this time the engine roared. He waited a few seconds and then slowly released the choke. The engine slowed but continued to turn over.

"Got it," he told Sal. "Pull the dinghy to the stern and tie it to a cleat. Leave enough line to give it some space."

Sal did as told and then went to the bow and untied the *Blackhawk* from the buoy. He shouted to Matteo, who began to slowly maneuver the boat out of the cluster of vessels.

Five minutes later, they coursed through the narrow inlet of the lagoon and out onto the mirror-like surface of Lake Michigan, where a thin fog obscured them from the view of anyone on the beach.

"Steer wide of Navy Pier and then turn up the Chicago River," Sal said. "No rush. Keep the speed just over walking. There's no need to draw attention."

"This is a powerful boat. I'd love to spend the day just cruising the lake," Matteo replied and smiled for the first time in weeks. He looked again at the fuel gauge—full. After they set fire to the planes, maybe he would just push Rizzo over the side and head for Michigan. He glanced at the compass; they were heading east. Michigan was northeast of Chicago. He'd find it, that he was sure of.

As they turned into the Chicago River and passed along Navy Pier, they noticed a few people walking about. A few delivery trucks were parked along the pier's length. Three men with fishing poles propped on a railing tested their luck. Further downriver, they passed under the Michigan Avenue Bridge, and the clatter of cars and trucks rattled over them. As they came out from the bridge's shadow, two people waved at them. Sal waved back.

"Pays to be cordial," he said.

Matteo said nothing; he was watching a large barge stacked with oilcans being towed out toward the lake. Behind it, a dozen other small boats busied themselves crisscrossing the river.

"Should be another mile or so," said Sal. "Everything looks so different from down here. We're looking for Harrison Street."

"They hang the street names from the bridge. That will make it easier," Matteo told him.

For ten more minutes, they slowly cruised downriver, passing under a half-dozen iron bridges. Tall, stone-faced, buildings climbed almost from the water's edge. In other places, they passed piers that jutted out into the river; a few had half-submerged abandoned boats tied to them. In the deep shadows under the bridges, they saw men huddled together over a morning fire. Matteo thought he could smell the aroma of coffee.

"Shitty way to live," he said, after they passed the third of such encampments.

"It's all due to the capitalists and industrialists. These are the people they discard when they don't need them anymore. Cavallo, we may be fighting the fascists, but it is the industrialists that we really need to stop. Even Mussolini is in the clutches of the capitalists and the almighty dollar."

"Or lira."

"Or the pound or the franc. Those who control the banks control everything."

For the most part, Matteo tried to ignore Sal's rant. Some of what his companion said had truth, but right now Matteo simply wanted to hide the boat and get this business over with.

A short wooden dock paralleled a narrow dirt road under the Harrison Street Bridge. A small tugboat was moored at one end. It's stern, partially submerged, had settled into the river.

"I'll turn the bow around," Matteo said. "It will make it easier to get back to the lake. I'll back her up against the dock. You jump and tie her up."

"You have a way of disabling this boat so we can be sure it will be here when we come back?" Sal asked.

"There are three fuses here"—Matteo pointed to the dashboard—"If I pull these out, no battery power goes to the motor. Will only take a minute to reinsert them. That should do it."

Holding a thick hemp line, Sal jumped from the boat and onto the dock. Matteo reversed the *Blackhawk* and expertly slid the boat against the dock and cut the engine.

Sal had found some tarps in the forward hold to lay over the stern and bow.

"That ought to cloak this boat from prying eyes," Sal said. "And let me hang onto the fuses."

LATER that morning Carla Acerbi watched Salvatore Rizzo pause at the top of the stairs and look up and down the narrow Chicago street. Not fifteen minutes earlier, she'd watched Rizzo and Matteo Cavallo return and enter the house from those same steps. Now only Cavallo remained inside. Rizzo lit a cigarette and then headed south on Wilton and hailed a taxi at the corner. The car headed west on Wrightwood Avenue.

Acerbi casually reached over to the footwell of the passenger-side seat and drew up a large canvas bag. She placed it on the seat and released the buckles that held the bag closed. She retrieved a small Mason jar, its lid tightly closed; inside was a wad of white cloth. After exiting the car, she slung the wide strap of the bag over her shoulder, locked the car, and then walked directly to the house that Rizzo had just left. Tight to her side, hidden between the bag and her hip, she held a fully loaded Luger.

The front door of the house was already open, and she used the butt of the pistol to tap on the frame of the screen door. She then slipped the pistol back into the bag, and with her free hand unscrewed the lid of the Mason jar.

"Who's there?" a voice yelled from inside the house.

"A friend. Rome sent me," Acerbi answered in Italian.

"I don't know anything about anyone in Rome," Cavallo said in English.

"I've come a long way."

"Leave now."

"Just a minute of your time. There's been a change. It's important."

"What? What change?" he asked, his voice sounding louder as he walked toward the door.

"Schedules. Are the others with you?"

"Sal just left. What schedules?"

Cavallo now stood at the door, just behind the screen. His eyes widened when he saw the woman just outside.

"I asked, what schedules? What do you know about what's going on?"

"I have the information here in my bag."

She made a show of poking about deep inside the canvas sack and withdrew a large folded file, the same file that Barbieri had given her.

"Here it is," she said, and held the file up to the screen. "All the information is here. May I come in? I brought this directly from Rome, from the professor at the university. It explains the need to change things, now that Balbo is late."

Cavallo opened the door a couple inches and stuck his hand out.

"Give it to me. I'll take a look."

"I can't let it out of my possession, sorry, but we can look it over inside."

She glanced around.

"I'm just a little too exposed out here."

She slid the file back into the bag.

Cavallo stared at Acerbi through the screen, trying to figure out what to do. Sal would know, but he'd gone to see Lucca and wouldn't be back for at least three hours. Shit, thought

Matteo. If it turned out to be important, he would need to dial Lucca's telephone number and talk to Sal.

"I guess it would be all right, sure," he said after a few more seconds.

He opened the door the rest of the way and Acerbi stepped inside.

"You didn't say your name."

"Donna Delucca. I work with the government's offices at the fair."

She looked around the dim interior; there was a strong smell of cigars and garlic. The entire house seemed to rattle as one of the elevated trains passed by directly behind it.

"How can you stand to live here with all that noise?"

"You get used to it, and the rent's cheap. What do you have for us?"

He started to walk toward the back of the house.

Acerbi removed the cloth from the Mason jar. As Cavallo walked slightly ahead of her, she dropped the bag and quickly wrapped her right arm around the man's throat. With her left, she slapped the cloth, heavy with its chloroform perfume, over his mouth. She held tightly onto his massive shoulders and neck while he bucked and twisted until the chemical did its work.

When he slumped to the floor, she rolled him over onto his back, leaving the cloth near his mouth so he would continue to draw in the fumes. She bound his feet and then his hands with a thin rope she took from her bag. Retrieving the small banner with its fascist symbol, she pushed it into Cavallo's mouth. She then quickly walked through the house. In the kitchen she saw a door and opened it; a flight of wooden stairs disappeared into the black basement.

She returned to the unconscious man and methodically worked him into a standing position, and then with one sweep of her strong arms, folded him over her shoulder. As she took him down the steps, she heard his head hit the plaster wall more than once. In the basement, she positioned him upright in a corner.

"Don't move, boy. If you do, I will be very angry."

Acerbi went back upstairs for one of the tubular steel chairs that surrounded the kitchen table; she chose the only one with arms. She also retrieved her bag. She spent the next ten minutes making Matteo Cavallo 'comfortable.' She tied his legs to the legs of the steel chair and his arms to the chrome arm rests. She then secured a length of silk rope around his thick neck with a knot that, as she pulled the rope, would not slip but continue to retain pressure against the man's neck. For the moment, she left the rope loose and walked around the basement, inspecting each shelf and labeled box. This was not nearly as interesting as the DeAngelos or Bovas' basements, but it was still fascinating. The things people kept in their basements—things they would probably never use or even think about again—continually amazed her. She turned back toward Cavallo when his muffled groans and coughs pushed their way past the gag.

"I see you are awake, excellent. If you continued to remain unconscious, it would be impossible to get the answers I need—so, good."

From the bag she retrieved a small glass vile and snapped off the top. The overpowering strength of ammonia filled the small room. She slipped the vial under Cavallo's nose; he started to choke, but his eyes noticeably brightened into a glare. He mumbled something.

"Sorry, I didn't understand," said his captor.

She held the Luger six inches from his face and removed the crushed banner.

"Now, what was it you said?"

"Go to fucking hell."

"Not helpful. Here's what I'm going to do, and I'm very

good at it. I will ask questions. If I think the answer you give is correct, I will only crush the little finger on your left hand. If the answer is wrong, I will crush the little finger on your right hand."

"You fascist bitch. I will tell you nothing."

"Signore Cavallo, everyone eventually tells me what I want to know. The real issue for you is time. Can you hold on long enough, hoping to be saved by Salvatore, or will you break and give me what I want before he comes back? Which leads me to my first question. Where is Lucca Barone? You have five seconds."

"Fuck you."

Before Cavallo could completely close his mouth Acerbi jammed the long muzzle of the pistol into his mouth. His front tooth broke from the impact. She then asked again, "Where is Barone? Is Rizzo with him?"

Cavallo violently shook his head from side to side, gagging as the muzzle probed against the back of his mouth.

Acerbi pulled the loose end of the rope against his throat, forcing him to stop his thrashing.

"Better," she said.

She loosened the rope and removed the Luger.

Cavallo took a deep, shaky breath.

"Now, please, answer my question."

"I don't know anyone named Lucca Barone."

"Wrong answer."

She reached back into her bag and pulled out a small sledgehammer.

The roaring and clattering of the elevated train, fifty feet behind the house, masked the sounds of Matteo Cavallo's screams to anyone passing by.

SAL burst through the door to Lucca's apartment. He held his revolver; his hands were shaking. He stared wordlessly at Maria, then at Lucca.

"Matteo is dead, murdered. No, no—God, he's been butchered," he said at last.

"What do you mean? He's dead?" Lucca asked.

"He was tied to a chair in the basement," Sal said, still shaking. "His throat cut from ear to ear. His hands were a mess, broken fingers, his face a bloody pulp."

Maria gasped.

Sal glared at her.

"If this ass here hadn't been so fucked-up in his head over you, he would have been there. He could have stopped it."

Suddenly, they were all yelling.

"He'd be dead too," Maria screamed. "It's those fools who sent you here. Did you think the fascists would just wait for you to blow up their airplanes? Did you think they would allow this to happen?"

"It's all your damned fault," Sal told her.

"It's like everything in Italy now. Il Duce has his ears to everything."

Her words only seemed to anger Sal more.

"It's over, Sal, over," Lucca yelled. "They know where you live. They probably followed you here. We need to stop this—now."

As if all at once exhausted, Sal slumped into a chair, the pistol dangling from his hand.

"We have to finish what we started," he said flatly. "You son of a bitch, you have no options. You have to help. That's why we were sent here. And if you refuse, I'll put a bullet through"—he twisted in his chair and pointed the gun at Maria—"her pretty little head. Do you understand, asshole?"

Lucca, his eyes wide, looked at Maria then at Sal.

"Put the gun down," he said quietly. "I'll help."

"No, Lucca, you can't," Maria pleaded. "You'll be killed. If they knew about Matteo, they will have security everywhere. You don't even know where the planes will be."

"They will be near Navy Pier, where else would they be?" Sal said. "The boat's ready. I watched Matteo, and I can get it out onto the lake. And, yes, you'll help. And to make sure, neither of you are leaving this basement until we are ready to load the boat."

23

THE WAIT WAS OVER. At six o'clock on Saturday evening, two hundred thousand Chicagoans and fair visitors lined the waterfront as General Italo Balbo and his twenty-four Savoia-Marchetti twin-engine seaplanes took a lazy turn over the city. In formations of three, the planes descended and landed alongside Navy Pier. Each time a plane landed, a roar went up from the crowd. After disembarking his own aircraft, Balbo waited in a small launch as each of his fellow aviators landed perfectly. It was almost anticlimactic after the months of anticipation.

It took an hour before Balbo stepped off the deck of the *USS Wilmette* and onto American soil. He waved to the excited and boisterous crowds. Some were disappointed because he'd arrived late and their individual celebrations had been canceled. Nonetheless, for the next few hours into the evening, it was as if he and his ninety-six airmen had been swept up into a Midwestern tornado as they were spun from one event and festivity to another. Sixty thousand people and dignitaries greeted them at Soldier Field that evening; everyone wanted to see Balbo. It was very late, many hours after sundown, when the team finally retired to their rooms at the Drake Hotel.

The seaplanes, after their 6,500-mile journey, were secured

to buoys spaced a few hundred feet apart, forming a U-shape in the harbor north of the Navy Pier. The lakefront was nearly overflowing with gawkers, well-wishers and tourists. Thirty years after the Wright brothers had launched their spruce-and-muslin-covered bi-wing contraption of an air machine, world leadership in design and construction of modern aircraft now belonged to the Italians. This adventure proved it, and Balbo's stage, the Chicago Century of Progress World's Fair, could not have been larger.

Until the flyers' scheduled departure on Wednesday to New York City, every day would be filled with parades, lunches, dinners, and tours of the impressive fairgrounds. A celebratory mass at Holy Name Cathedral would be officiated by the archbishop. There would be the unveiling of the Christopher Columbus statue and many other honors. The mayor and the city would even rename Seventh Street, a few blocks from the Congress Hotel, as Balbo Drive.

Acerbi leaned against a tree in the narrow park squeezed between Lake Shore Drive and the beach and watched as Balbo and his planes dropped onto the lake. She was leery of crowds; they were unpredictable. Somewhere in the mass of joyous celebrants was Salvatore Rizzo. She knew he had to be here, plotting and figuring his next move. The seaplanes were his targets; of that she was now sure. Somehow, during the next two evenings, Rizzo and his remaining conspirator would try an attack. She guessed they would come from the river. A boat would be used. Maybe they would use grenades, maybe fire. They would have to move fast from airplane to airplane. She was sure the mission would be suicidal. She would start on the Chicago River as soon as it got dark. They had to be on the river. She would find them—she had to find them—and she would stop them.

OFFICALLY, Saturday and Sunday were Alfano's days off. The department's budget was tight, so tight that overtime was seldom permitted. But Balbo's arrival changed all that, schedules were thrown out. The mayor made sure, especially after their conversation, that Alfano stayed on the job. Alfano enjoyed watching the landings from an open vantage point along Michigan Avenue near the Drake Hotel. The seaplanes passed in formation along the waterfront. Above them flew the cadre of Army Air Corp planes that had acted as escort from Detroit. Alfano stood by the Packard and lit a cigarette and wondered what it would be like to fly. The highest off the ground he'd been was on the day he chased a killer onto the Sky Ride at the local fair. He'd been too busy trying not to die to appreciate the view.

So tonight or tomorrow it would happen, or not. If he and McDunnah were right, everything was now in motion. The major performer had made a grand theatrical entry. The stage was set; all that remained were the individual players— and it was Tony's job to figure out who those players were. He crushed the cigarette on the sidewalk and climbed back into the Packard. It was late, and he was very sure he would not be getting much sleep over the next few days. He drove through the crowded streets to his apartment, stopping to pick up a slice of prime rib, a baked potato, salad and the famous dinner rolls from Henrici's on Randolph Street. A bottle of Chianti was also slipped into the bag.

The Kowalski apartment was dark; no doubt they were out watching the festivities. Tired and hungry, Alfano felt thankful for the small favor of not having to deal with their drama as he climbed up to his apartment. He'd decided to look for a new apartment, something closer to the station, maybe something a little nicer. In the vicinity of Taylor Street, near some of his favorite Italian restaurants. Our Lady of Pompeii wasn't a bad parish; there were good people, people he understood, and

Father Remigio Pigato, the new pastor, was a good man. Yes, moving would be a good idea.

He reheated his dinner on the small electric hot plate, turned on WGN radio and listened to the announcer give minute-by-minute accounts of Balbo and the dignitaries at Soldier Field. Alfano had had enough of Soldier Field to last a lifetime. For a moment he thought maybe there would be a bomb, like on opening day. He put that notion out his mind. Too much thinking and too much wine could make a guy paranoid—or more paranoid. Alfano was cynical and paranoid enough for three men. He filled his glass again, changed the station to a jazz combo that was playing in a ballroom of a Kansas City hotel, and enjoyed his steak.

Maybe this is all that it will ever be, listening to jazz, drinking wine, wishing for the old days of bad guys and cheap liquor. Fuck, it could be worse.

As he cleaned the dishes, he heard the Kowalskis arrive. Her voice pierced the quiet; Alfano couldn't hear what she said, only that it was loud and strained. Mr. Kowalski's loud and defiant bass drum of a voice answered. Whatever was going on was escalating. Alfano hated domestic rows; they never accomplished anything, and more than once during the last twenty years he'd lost a fellow cop to some drunken husband with a gun.

He downed his glass of wine and went to the door. The shouting was now in the stairway.

"What the hell's going on?" Alfano demanded, as he swung open the door. "What the devil are you two screaming about?"

Both Kowalskis looked up at him. Alice Kowalski's face instantly turned red.

"It's nothing, Detective. Nothing really," Mr. Kowalski offered.

"Didn't sound like nothing."

"We was having an argument about the Italians, those guys

that landed this afternoon," Alice said. "This fool says that Balbo is a good fascist and is helping Italy."

She pointed at her husband.

"I said that men like him and his buddies would as soon cut your throat if you got in their way. They are nothing but thugs in fancy uniforms. Obviously, this Polack hasn't a clue about modern politics and what's going on in the world. And him a good union man—I'd say he's got his priories all in a jumble. You tell him, Mr. Alfano. You tell him the true story."

"Good God, you two. Is this what all the yelling's been about? I thought you were about to kill each other."

"Kill each other?" Mr. Kowalski said, genuinely surprised. "Hardly, even though she's as hardheaded as they come."

"I prefer stubborn," Alice put in.

"Whatever it is, just stop it. I'm tired and with these airplane jockeys in town, it's only going to get crazier. So lower the volume, okay?"

"Yes, sir, Detective," Mr. Kowalski said. "Sorry."

"Not a problem, and to both of your concerns, I think we are in the early stages of what will turn out to be an epic battle between the communists and fascists that will make our little Chicago gang wars look like fist fights on the playground. There's a lot going on, and we will have very little to say about it. So go to bed and for Pete's sake, try and be quiet."

As Alfano closed his door, his phone began to ring.

24

"WE HAVE ANOTHER ONE," McDunnah said. "The sergeant on the scene says very messy, near the North Side, on Milton near Wrightwood."

"Thanks, just what we need. You stay there, Sergeant. You need to be my ears and eyes. Put up a few more posters on the murder board. Maybe you can find a better picture of General Balbo."

The scene in the basement of the house on Milton Street was becoming familiar. For once Alfano had arrived before the coroner and now stood looking at the lifeless victim tied to a chair, this time a young man, head back, eyes open, blood covering his upper body, his hands looking like hamburger.

"Did someone call this in?" Alfano asked the sergeant, who stood off to one side.

"Yes, one hour ago. I was first on the scene with Danny there. Quite a shock."

"Did the caller leave a name?"

"No, only the address—and it was a woman's voice. We haven't had time to look around."

"Coroner?"

"On his way. The traffic is all fouled up due to the Italians landing. What a mess."

"Not as much as what's here," said Alfano. "Anything more about this woman caller, her voice?"

"None, though the desk sergeant who took the call said she had an Italian accent."

"Shit, it had to be the murderer."

"A woman?" the sergeant asked.

"Yes, damn it, a woman."

Alfano looked through everything spread about the basement: a short piece of thin cord lay on the floor beneath the chair. He knew it would turn out to be silk. Why the escalation to cutting the kid's throat, he wasn't sure. He climbed the stairs to the kitchen. A stack of envelopes lay on the counter. He read the names: Salvatore Rizzo, Matteo Cavallo. These two were receiving mail at the Milton address. Two of the envelopes had Loyola College on the return address. Which one of the two men was in the basement, he wasn't sure.

"Thought I'd find you here," Abrahamson said, when he walked into the kitchen. "Like the others?"

"Yes, but worse. This fellow had his throat cut after all the preliminaries."

"Shit. I'll let you know what I find after the autopsy."

As Alfano walked back out to the street, the squealing of metal wheels from the elevated train behind the house interrupted the quiet of the late evening. The sergeant's patrol car, the coroner's van, and his Packard were parked in front of the house. Neighbors stood in small groups on the opposite side of the narrow street, craning for a look as Alfano came out. He scanned the faces; no one looked out of the ordinary or as if they didn't belong. A cluster of kids, he guessed no more than ten years old, stood well away from the adults, talking among themselves. He walked over to them.

"You fellows know who lives there?"

He flashed his star.

One of the boys took a step forward.

"Yeah, maybe."

"Maybe what? You know who lives there?"

"Couple of dagos," the kid answered.

"You mean Italians?"

"Yeah, Italians. What happened?"

"Something not nice. One of them is dead."

"No shit," one of the other boys said.

"Watch your language," Alfano said. "Anything funny happen around here recently?"

"Funny? What do you mean, funny?"

"Strange, different. You guys seem to know what happens around here, so did you see anything strange?"

The boys looked at each other, avoiding Alfano's eyes.

"Well?"

"You tell him, Tommy," one of the boys said. "You talked to her."

"Talked to whom?"

The boy, Tommy—the one who'd spoken up first—stood fidgeting under Alfano's gaze.

"Well maybe there was something, but I'm so squealer," the boy said at last.

"Never said you were. What happened?"

"Well, a couple of days ago this woman was parked out front here, actually up the street a bit. So's I asked her what she was doing, and she said she was a P.I. and that she was watching these guys. Told us to keep quiet about it. She was a looker."

"What do you know about a looker?" Alfano asked.

"I's know good-looking women, and she was one of 'em. Smart mouth, too. Said she'd knock us off we said anything. So we didn't."

"Anything else?"

Sounding more confident, Tommy said that the woman had been driving a late-model sedan and had stayed about an hour, then left.

"An Oldsmobile, new," he told Alfano. "Great car."

Alfano nearly smiled when the boy added that such a car was "a little too high hat for the neighborhood."

"You get a license number?" he asked Tommy.

To his amazement, the boys had scrawled the number on a scrap of paper.

"Tell him the rest," one of the gang said.

"Well, she came back a couple of times, was here late morning today. Billy here saw her go into the house, carrying a large bag. She left in about an hour. Not seen her since."

25

AFTER SMOKING a cigarette out on the sidewalk, Salvatore Rizzo walked back into the basement apartment, where Lucca and Maria were tied to chairs in the small kitchen, gags over their mouths. The young woman's eyes were narrow with hatred.

"I'll untie you, Barone, if you promise to remain calm. I don't want to hurt your girlfriend. Do I have your promise?"

Lucca looked at Maria. She nodded. Rizzo removed Lucca's gag and loosened the ropes around his arms.

"Was all this necessary? Christ, Sal, we've been together on this for almost half a year. I wouldn't turn you in."

"It's not you. It's her."

Maria's expression had not changed, but she also understood the futility of her position. She mumbled something through her gag.

"Can I take her gag off?"

"Sure, why not."

"You're fucking crazy, Rizzo, crazy," Maria said, spitting out bits of the cloth. "Walk away from all this."

Rizzo ignored her.

"I saw Balbo's airplanes," he told Lucca. "The security is the shits, and with the crowds and all the chaos, it will be easy to get near them. They are tied to buoys next to Navy Pier. Just about where we thought they would be. Maybe a hundred feet between them, and just a couple of patrol boats on the lake."

Lucca said nothing.

"So, Barone, are you going to help? We need to get these cans down to the river, and I need you to drive the boat while I dump the gasoline."

"Rizzo, I won't let you take him," Maria said. "This is crazy. You're crazy. It's suicide."

"I don't fucking care."

Rizzo turned again to Lucca.

"The truck is out front. We'll load the cans, drive to the boat and put them on board. We'll be done in less than an hour."

"Whoever killed Matteo probably knows who you are," Maria said. "Why do you think they tortured him?"

"It's been hours, we should be dead then. No, he didn't tell them," Sal told her. "Buys us a little time. And all the more reason to get started."

He pointed the gun at her, then slowly turned it on Lucca.

"Are you going to do your duty?"

"I'll go, but she stays here," Lucca answered.

"No way. Where you go, I go," Maria said. "Six hands are better than four."

"Promise, on your mother's life?" Rizzo asked her.

"Promise."

It took less than ten minutes to load the cans into the back of the truck and cover them with a heavy green tarp. Maria, with Rizzo still holding his revolver on her, drove down Taylor Street to Canal Street, then to the Harrison Street pier. The sounds of revelers punctuated the night as they passed one bar after another along the main street of Little Italy. It was a night of celebration, and a good night to be Italian.

At Rizzo's direction, Maria turned off Harrison Street and down a narrow gravel road that swung under the bridge. The boat, still covered with tarps, looked undisturbed.

"Could someone have messed with it?" Lucca said.

He grabbed two of the gas cans.

"All's good," Sal replied after a quick glance around.

If anyone had tried to get onboard, they would have had to open the gate in the railing, he told them. He had tied a string between the gate and the railing. The string was still there, unbroken.

He held up the fuses that Matteo had earlier removed.

"And besides, I have these," he said. "Without them, the boat will go nowhere."

Lucca did not argue. Sal was a fool. There were doubtless ways of getting onto the boat without breaking the string, but an argument would gain them nothing.

The two men each made eight trips, carrying the cans. Lucca told Maria to stop after four trips; she looked exhausted. Each can weighed about forty-five pounds and had to be carried down a slippery narrow gravel path to the pier. Maria stood to one side and watched as Lucca and Sal climbed back up the hill to the truck for their last trip. She eyed Sal's revolver, tucked inside his belt so it was snug against his back. As the two men started back down the trail, she moved to the end of the pier and waited while Sal told Lucca the plan.

"Here's what we're going to do. You will drive the boat where I tell you. When we near the first of the planes, I'll empty the can under the plane. The gas floats on top of the water. When we get to the next plane, I'll fire a flare at the first. When it explodes, we will be on to the third. We keep doing this until we have emptied all the cans."

"We'll be caught as soon as the first plane catches fire."

"No, they will be looking at the fire and a burning plane. They will think it's an accident. These planes are made of wood and heavy canvas; they will burn like a Roman candle. We can stay ahead of them. We may not get all the planes but even if it's just one, it will embarrass Balbo and Mussolini and will make our point."

Sal leaned down and set the last cans into the stern of the boat. As he turned away from Maria, she grabbed the revolver from his belt. Rizzo spun back around and tried to grab the gun. Maria fired, just missing his shoulder, but the bullet nicked his earlobe.

"Shit, what the hell's this for?"

Rizzo put his hand against the edge of his ripped and bleeding ear. Blood dripped onto his shoulder.

"We have to do this," he said, his voice almost plaintive.

"No, you don't, Rizzo," Maria said calmly. "Lucca, get behind me."

Lucca slowly moved away from Rizzo.

"Is this how it's going to be, Barone?" Rizzo yelled. "You now a coward, a fool, all because of some bitch of a woman?"

"Shut up, Rizzo, or I will put the next one between your eyes," Maria said. "And I do know how to use this. So forget about trying anything stupid, even though I would expect it. Lucca and I are leaving. You can do what you want with all this gasoline, I really don't care. Maybe there will be an accident or maybe Matteo's killer is waiting for you. It is all yours now. We are going."

She held the revolver steady with two hands, the barrel pointed directly at his face.

After a few long seconds, Rizzo backed away slowly and climbed over the gunnel of the boat. He headed to the bridge, replaced the fuses, and started the engine. It roared to life and within seconds softened to a steady rumble with an occasional gurgle from the exhaust. He walked to the stern. His eyes never left Maria.

"This is a great thing we are doing, can't you see that?" he said holding a cloth he'd found in the bridge to the side of his face.

"Can't you see that it's not worth Matteo's life and your life? It's stupid," Maria said. "Mussolini will still go on. He will fuck over his people whether you blow up his planes or not. It doesn't mean a thing."

"Yes, it—"

Rizzo's retort was drowned out by the sound of a gunshot from overhead. The sound echoed through the understory of the iron bridge. Maria spun on her heels as a nearby lamppost exploded and a shard of wood impaled in her cheek. Lucca jerked his gaze up to the bridge deck; a woman looked down over the railing, a pistol in her hand. He turned back to Maria. Blood was running down her cheek, an inch away from her eye. She collapsed as he grabbed her. With Maria tucked under his arm, he whirled around as another report from the pistol kicked up a cloud of dust inches from his right knee. The engine of the motor launch roared. Lucca watched Rizzo hurriedly cast off the lines from the pier and turn the boat into the current of the Chicago River.

The woman above them screamed and fired again. Another slug embedded itself in the ground near Lucca. All he could do was shield Maria with his body as four more shots rang out.

"What?" he whispered, when Maria mumbled something.

"Leave me, get out of here. She will kill both of us."

"Not a chance. She's after Rizzo and the boat."

As if in confirmation, they heard a car engine start overhead.

"I think she's going to try and stop him, whoever the hell she is," Lucca said.

He gently touched Maria's cheek, and she grabbed his bloody hand and squeezed.

"It stings, but I'll be okay."

"You caught a splinter in the cheek. It's just a little blood.

That's good, but I have to get you to a hospital."

He looked up the trail toward the truck, then moved as if to carry her.

"No hospital, too many questions, and I can walk," she said.

"We'll go back to my apartment," Lucca said. "I have some things there."

They slowly climbed the trail, listening to be sure the shooter had departed.

"There are at least a dozen bridges Sal has to pass under," Lucca whispered. "She could wait for him at each of them and hope for a lucky shot."

Maria stumbled, and he pulled her closer.

"Here, keep applying pressure," he said.

She pushed his handkerchief against the wound, she flinched. He helped her into the cab of the truck. They could hear the sound of the escaping boat echoing amongst the buildings that flanked the river.

26

LUCK HAD SMILED, albeit somewhat wryly, on Carla Acerbi this night. Matteo Cavallo had admitted that a boat was tied to a pier on the Chicago River, ready to be loaded with the cans of gasoline he and his cohorts intended to use to sabotage Italo Balbo's seaplanes. However, the fool couldn't remember what the name of the bridge was. His total lack of knowledge about the city's street and bridges only added to her urgency. She knew this had to be the night that Rizzo and his people would attack; there was no other logical option. Balbo and his crew were being celebrated and feted with dinners, political speeches and honors.

After extracting from Cavallo all she could, including his life, all she could do was crisscross the Chicago River bridges in her automobile, looking for some sign that the communists were lurking. She started at the Lake Street Bridge and worked her way south, one bridge at a time. She crossed the Randolph Street and Washington Street Bridges, then over the bridges named after the other American presidents: Madison, Monroe and Adams, periodically stopping to get out and scan the shoreline below for signs of Rizzo's boat. When she turned off Canal Street she stopped in the middle of the Harrison Street Bridge, got out and looked over the side. One streetlight atop a wooden pole barely lit the area, but a break in the thick foliage under the bridge allowed a quick view of two men carrying something heavy in the semi-darkness.

She then caught the voice of a woman yelling at someone under the bridge. She stared hard at the shadowy figures. There was a flash of light she recognized as muzzle flash, accompanied by the unmistakable sound of a gunshot. Moving down the bridge to get a better view, she heard the engine of a boat start. She reacted by raising her pistol and waiting. When a woman stepped into her line of view, Acerbi fired. Then a man showed; as he bent near the woman, Acerbi fired again and again. The couple disappeared in the shadows. She heard the motor of the launch roar from under the bridge and ran to the opposite side just as the motorboat emerged. She fired four times at where she thought the driver of the boat should be; the boat didn't slow.

She sprinted back to her car. The tires squealed on the metal grill of the bridge deck as she spun the car around to follow the boat upriver to Lake Michigan. The only way to stop the boat would be to intercept it as it passed under one of the dozen bridges that crossed the river between here and the lake. She had only one goal: complete her mission. That translated into a single objective: kill whoever was driving that boat.

"THE PLANES ARE ONLY ON THE LAKE FOR TWO MORE DAYS," Alfano said to McDunnah. "If it happens, it will be tonight or tomorrow. With too many things to potentially go wrong, my guess, they'll try tonight to gain some advantage."

The sergeant looked thoughtful.

"What a disaster for the city, the mayor and the Italian community," he said. "It's a proud week for your people. To have those planes attacked would be more than humiliating."

"So let's see what we can do to stop it."

McDunnah looked at his pocket watch.

"It's almost midnight. Too late to get our people out on the water in any organized way," he said.

"You're right. Hell, half the police force is out guarding General Balbo. Who do we have left?"

"I'll call the city's fireboat," McDunnah said, "and tell them we'll be boarding in ten minutes."

"For God's sake, tell them someone is trying to blow up the seaplanes. That should get their attention."

Nine minutes later, Alfano and McDunnah climbed aboard the fireboat *Graeme Stewart*. The pilot eased the vessel out of its mooring at the Franklin Street pier and into the Chicago River. Alfano briefed the boat captain on what might happen.

"Well, we needed an exercise anyway," the captain said. "Do you have any idea where they might come from?"

"None. But we do know they can only be heading to one spot—that's where those twenty-four seaplanes are moored. You were out there when the planes arrived?"

The captain nodded.

"Yes, and what a spectacle," he said. "Each landing was as pretty as a mallard on a pond, one after the other. We had our hoses up, shooting water more than fifty feet into the air. My men were proud, real proud."

The captain suggested they head out to the end of Navy Pier toward the seaplanes and watch for any boats that might approach. The boats would be visible with the lights of the city as a backdrop.

"And if the worst happens, we can be there to stop them," he said.

The pilot maneuvered into the channel of the Chicago River and headed toward the open water of Lake Michigan. They passed the new skyscraper edifice of the Jewelers Building, where Mary Ann DeAngelo had spent her last working hours, then under the Wacker Avenue Bridge, where Alfano's old captain had been found dead after the *Tribune* tower bombing. Ahead, the iconic Michigan Avenue Bridge loomed over the river.

CARLA ACERBI raced the three blocks to the Monroe Street Bridge, the next crossing of the Chicago River ahead of the saboteur's boat. The night was warm, the lights from the high-rise buildings danced off the river, no other boats moved up or down the waterway. It had to be the man called Sal, she reasoned. Lucca was the kid with the girl, so the one in the boat must be Rizzo.

Once at the bridge and on alert, she replaced the clip in her Luger and patted her jacket and felt the two back-ups. Should be enough, had to be enough. She looked up and down the street. This late at night, even the cross-town traffic had stopped. It was as if the city had shut down. Only one lonesome cab and a newspaper truck passed her on the bridge. She waited.

Sal Rizzo gripped the wheel of the launch with his left hand while he felt for the small .38 revolver in his pant's pocket. He'd doused every light on the console, hoping to improve his visibility as he headed upriver toward the lake. Who the hell had been shooting at them? It had to be the ones who'd killed Cavallo. He'd been warned about potential assassins, killers sent by Mussolini and the fascists. Killers who would do anything to stop them.

"If you are caught, don't tell them anything. Better yet don't get caught," his handlers had cautioned.

It was obvious that Cavallo hadn't followed that order. Because of him, the operation was now in chaos. And not being able to keep his fucking mouth shut had gotten him killed.

Rizzo stared into the crisscross of bridges ahead that provided some semblance of a roof over the river—he'd lost count since leaving Barone and his girlfriend on the riverbank, but he thought there must be four or five more bridges before the turn to the lake. He scanned from one side of the river to the other. Headlights from the few cars about reflected off the buildings and the water. Back and forth, back and forth, he stared into the dark places that lined the river.

A movement on the next bridge, two hundred feet ahead, caught his eye. In the center of the span stood someone silhouetted against the windows of the office buildings beyond. It was probably nothing, just a bum walking the bridge. Before he had time to revise that opinion, a hole appeared in the windshield. The first shot landed about a foot to his left, followed by another and another until the windscreen failed, spraying shattered glass at him and around him. Pieces of glass shredded his hands; he felt a sharp pain in his cheek. Looking back at the street bridge, he saw another flash and heard the slug hit near the floor in the rear section of the boat's bridge. He threw the throttle into full, not caring now whether the police were around or would pay attention. The boat zoomed under the bridge, and for a moment was safe from rounds fired from above.

It had to be them. Shit.

He wished to God he could make the boat stop directly under the bridge, but momentum and speed carried him quickly under and then out from the relative safety of the bridge's underside. Once again visible to the assailant above, he looked ahead to the hopeful safety of the onrushing bend in the river.

He felt the impacts of more slugs hitting the wall of the bridge behind him. Probing shots that sliced through the thin mahogany paneling like hot rivets into butter. He fishtailed the boat across the surface, hoping to redirect the aim of the shooter. Then he heard the stacked cans of gasoline tumble and fall to the deck. He'd forgotten about the hundreds of gallons of gasoline not twenty feet behind him.

"SHIT, WHAT THE HELL WAS THAT?" Sergeant Mc-Dunnah said, turning and pointing back up the river.

Carving its way toward them was a motor launch, entirely engulfed in flames. Unstoppable, its speed easily doubled the speed of the lumbering fireboat. It seemed to be aimed directly at them.

"Helmsman, pull to port," the captain yelled, then to the crew on the stern, "Ready the water canons. Get the pumps running!"

The motor launch raced toward them. Flames more than twenty-feet high billowed like angry orange balloons in its wake. Dozens of onlookers had gathered along the railings of the Michigan Avenue Bridge. The boat and the flames headed directly at them.

"How the hell do we stop that?" the helmsman screamed. "In a second, she'll pass us."

Alfano heard and felt the massive pumps in the bowels of the fireboat spin into life. The first powerful streams of water arched toward the onrushing launch.

"Ram her, Captain," Alfano yelled. "Drive her into the wall. God knows what will happen if it gets to the rail yard."

"Helm, you heard the detective. Ram that boat," said the captain.

The helmsman looked back up the river. The engulfed launch was less than a hundred yards behind them. He estimated he had ten seconds to make the maneuver. He turned to starboard a degree then eased the bow directly into the path of the onrushing boat. He just missed the enflamed gunnel, and the chance to ram it into the vertical concrete wall along the riverfront. All that the men on the fireboat could see to their starboard side was a wall of flames. Thousands of gallons of water from the canons deluged the launch, nearly capsizing her, but she quickly uprighted and raced on. The bow of the fireboat was momentarily engulfed in flames, then the fireboat was left churning in the wake of the escaping inferno.

"Fuck," was all Alfano could say, as he watched the launch race onward under the Michigan Avenue Bridge. He heard the screams of the people on the bridge as they ran to either end of the iron structure. Flames erupted through the open metal grating of the bridge then, just as quickly, moved on as the boat raced out toward the lake.

Just before it reached the lake, the inferno seemed to unbelievably intensify, as if hell had opened a doorway to allow the launch to enter. Suddenly, everything was no more. The massive explosion ripped the wooden boat into a million flaming shards and splinters. The sound was deafening. Moments later, all that remained drifting on the river was a thick pall of smoke and patches of fire that slowly floated out onto the lake.

"Jesus, Mary and Joseph," was all Sergeant McDunnah could say as he crossed himself.

27

SAL RIZZO swam the thirty yards to a dock secured to the riverbank, tilting his head after each stroke to watch the flaming yacht as it headed out onto Lake Michigan. He tensed after each pull of his arms, waiting for the impact of a bullet. When he made it to the riverbank, he stayed low and in the shadows, then took cover in the darkness of the concrete bulkhead that paralleled the river.

He watched as the massive fireball—the mahogany and chrome toy of a rich man from Racine—exploded into the sky. Billowing clouds of flame and smoke seem to engulf the people standing and gawking at the railings, but then he realized the explosion was beyond the Michigan Avenue Bridge.

Now, maybe they will think I'm dead. I can only fucking hope?

It had gone wrong, horribly wrong. Matteo must have told them everything, even where to find the boat. Rizzo sat against the wall with his knees up and his arms wrapped around his legs, listening. Blood from his torn ear dripped on his wet sleeve, he ripped off part of the shirt and used it to stem the flow. Maybe they hadn't seen him dive off the burning boat, maybe they would think he was hit by a lucky bullet, maybe they'd think he'd drowned or had been blown into a million chunks of burning flesh. He didn't care who they were. He retrieved the small revolver from his pocket, glad it had not sunk to the bottom of the river. All he cared about now was escape.

THE SON of a bitch had to be dead; no one could survive that explosion.

It made no difference; her work was done. In three days, the general and his squadron would be gone and Carla Acerbi could go home. The security around the seaplanes would be impossible for even a duck to get near.

She poured herself another glass of wine. The bottles the embassy had placed in her apartment were excellent Barolos and Chiantis as well as a few chardonnays from regions north of Venice. She now waited for a delivery from the small Italian restaurant she'd frequented during her time here.

On the table were train tickets and passage on the ocean liner *Rex* back to Naples acquired by Barbieri.

Let the fool believe what he wants, there are many ways to get home to Italy.

An hour earlier, she'd stood and watched as the boat sped out into the lake and exploded. She reckoned that at least for tonight, it was over. There would be no further attempts on the fleet of seaplanes. She was also confident that the driver of the boat, Sal Rizzo, was dead. That was the name the fool Cavallo had screamed out as she systematically broke his fingers. Sal Rizzo and Lucca Barone. The woman she'd seen with Barone intrigued her. Even in the dark, she had recognized her from somewhere. It had come to her when she'd glanced toward the end of the bridge, where a one-story high billboard above Wacker Boulevard advertised the Century of Progress Fair.

Of course, the cute Italian girl in the exhibition hall. Quite nice, very pretty, naïve, maybe even delicious.

Acerbi had driven through the city on the way back to her apartment, passing thousands of people crowding onto the pedestrian walks of the bridges that led to the lake. She was glad that she didn't have to cross any of the bridges to head north. They were jammed with people, gawking and pointing at the river. She found an open spot on Hubbard Street, parked and walked the block to the Michigan Avenue Bridge. Below, on the river, a dozen small watercraft milled about a large fireboat that still streamed arcs of water at the burning debris from the exploded boat.

"What happened?" she asked a gentleman standing at the railing.

"Haven't a clue. Someone said a boat, entirely on fire, was heading out toward the lake and then exploded. Me, I was a few blocks away, but sure as hell heard it and saw the fireball."

"Were there people on board?"

"No one seems to know. But boats like that—people are saying it was an expensive yacht—got to have a crew. Don't know myself; it's just a lot of crap in the water now. God rest their souls if they were on board."

Acerbi turned away and walked back to her car.

"God rest his fucking soul," she said aloud, to no one in particular.

LUCCA sat smoking a cigarette in the small front room of the basement apartment. The one double-hung window looked out onto a dirty alley. He poured a second glass of wine. The stench of the gasoline had all but dissipated.

"I've lied to you," he said, stroking Maria's cheek.

"Why?" she answered.

"I guess to protect you, but now I think it's because I'm pissed at myself for getting involved with all of this. Others have died. Matteo has died, and now probably Sal."

"Who was that woman? Why did she want to kill us?"

"I think she was sent to stop us. Other than that, I don't know who she is."

Lucca then explained everything to Maria: why he was in America, the plan to sabotage the seaplanes and foil Italo Balbo.

"All this to embarrass Mussolini, when the fool himself

does that better than his enemies? Your attempt would only infuriate him," she said.

"It was all to be a protest against the fascists and all that Mussolini is doing to destroy Italy. In time, the monster will have us at war."

"Right now, if they know about Matteo and Sal, they will try to find you."

"Me? I'm okay. I'll find an apartment somewhere in Cicero or the South Side and hide out for a while."

"You mean us. I'm going with you."

"Not a chance, not until this is over. You have to stay away from me. With me you might be killed—and that is not going to happen."

The sound of someone stumbling down the stair just outside the apartment startled both of them. Lucca put a finger to his lips. He reached across the table and picked up Sal's revolver.

The knock was soft, almost pleading. It came again, more insistent.

Gun in his hand, Lucca stood to the side of the door and asked, "Who's there?" then waited. The knock came again. He asked louder.

"Sal, it's Sal."

Maria opened the door and stared.

"You alone?" she asked.

"Yes."

As Sal stumbled into the room, he spied the bottle of wine. He quickly took a slug directly from the bottle. Then another.

"Better?" Maria said, looking at the pistol in Lucca's hand.

"What the hell are you doing here?" Lucca demanded. "Matteo knew about this place. He could have talked. They could be here any minute. We need to get out."

"I couldn't agree more, but they've had time. They would have already been here if they knew, " Maria said. "I have a cousin on the South Side. He can hide us for a few days until we can figure all of this out."

"What's to figure?" Sal said. "They found out, they were waiting. They have to be the ones that killed Matteo, and whoever it is won't stop until we are dead."

"It was a woman. Just before she turned to cross the bridge, I saw her face," Maria said. "I saw her at the pavilion once. She was the one shooting at us. She's the one who blew up your boat."

"At the pavilion? Where you work?" Lucca asked.

"I think so. It certainly looked like her—she's the one I told you about, the creepy one. If this is connected to the people at the fair, it is all a fool's errand," Maria said. "Now you have nothing, and you lost your friend. There's not much else you can do."

"I could try to assassinate Balbo," Sal said. "Maybe walk up and shoot him in the eye."

"You are a fool," Maria told him, not hiding her irritation. "Right now he is more protected than the mayor. After all this, it won't be too long before they figure out it was an attempt at sabotage. There will be dozens of boats guarding the seaplanes. Lick your wounds and leave this all alone."

"I can't. We were given a task. I intend to carry it out."

Lucca said, "Nothing will be gained, and anything that may get Maria hurt or killed—I will not let that happen."

Sal finished the bottle with one more gulp, then politely asked if there was another. Lucca pointed to the small kitchen area and the bottles stacked under the cabinets.

"Good," said Sal. "I'd hate to think we would run out."

28

IT WAS SUNDAY morning when Alfano and McDunnah headed back to Racine Street. The sun rose orange and angry over Lake Michigan, promising another hot and humid day. As they drove to the station, they passed more than a dozen soup lines queued along the length of many of Chicago's streets. Men, some with heads high and dignified, others just glad to put something in their bellies, scuffled together in disheveled congregations, hoping for a bite of breakfast.

McDunnah drove the Packard; Alfano sat on the passenger's side, watching the lines of human tragedies that flanked both sides of the street.

"I'm surprised that we don't have more trouble," McDunnah said. "All these unemployed and down-and-outs just looking for a chance. If things don't improve, there will be a revolution. I can taste it."

"Hungry men will fight for a meal. That's the way it was ten years ago when Mussolini took power. Get the men out of the soup line, give them something to do, someone to follow and they can take over a country."

"Like that Hitler fellow Germany just put in power?" added McDunnah.

"Yeah, desperate people will do anything to eat and take

care of their families; a desperate country will do anything to survive. Take Roosevelt—I wonder what he thinks he can do, everything is so fucked up. Maybe he can get something done. He sure stopped the run on the banks in March—what a way to become president. Something's going to have to be done with these poor fellows; the communists are already making noise. I just wonder where we'll end up."

"Two steps on the way to perdition is my guess," Mc-Dunnah said. "They didn't call them the Roaring Twenties for nothing. Now that was quite a time. This Depression is our penance."

"The twenties weren't that great. How many dead gangsters did we find on the streets in this town, compliments of Al Capone, Frank Nitti, the Irish gangs, and the Jews?"

"And politicians. You forgot politicians."

"Yeah, them too. But we did get Louis Armstrong, jazz, Gershwin, radio, airplanes . . ."

"That's enough, you win. But I still say we are a long way from anything normal."

"What's normal these days, McDunnah? When you figure that out, let me know."

Back at the station, the crime board changed again. Mc-Dunnah added a sketch of a burning speedboat to the wall.

"Nice drawing, a real da Vinci. You think this had something to do with the murders?" Alfano asked.

"Maybe. We have this Donna Delucca broad, who seems to be our killer. We have at least seven dead: the five Italians, one nightclub owner, and one possible hooker. And today and the next two days, we have an important fascist general being courted all over town after flying in with his seaplanes from Italy. After last night, to top it all, we have a blazing and exploding speedboat that may have been heading to those planes and maybe a guy or guys on the boat. Sounds like they might be tied together, if you ask me."

"If you put it that way, yes."

Alfano pointed to one of the names on the board.

"This Matteo Cavallo, killed the same way as the others. His body found in the basement of his house, and the report came in anonymously. His identification has him recently from Rome."

"Yeah, a student at Loyola. Maybe he was sent here to blow up the planes. The timing works."

"Maybe," Alfano offered, "but that would be a hard job for a single man to tackle."

"The speedboat says he had at least one other person helping him."

"Who is possibly dead."

"We've got lots of maybes here," the sergeant said. "Too many maybes."

"Tomorrow morning, I'll go up to Loyola admissions. If this fellow Cavallo was from Rome, it's a good bet that the others may have come with him. If we can get names, maybe we can get addresses."

Alfano's phone rang; McDunnah picked it up. He listened for a few seconds, then handed the receiver to Alfano.

"You don't want to take this."

ALFANO walked the oriental carpet that covered the tile floor of the mayor's receiving room. He was one very pissed-off Italian. Ever since General Balbo had landed on Lake Michigan, Alfano had only wanted a few minutes to take in the events, and parades, and celebrations honoring this hero of Italy. He was pissed because he'd spent his time chasing down a murderer and trying to stop someone from, maybe, blowing up Balbo's seaplanes. He was pissed because the mayor had summoned him to his office on twenty minutes notice. He was pissed at the mayor's uptight secretary. He lit a cigarette and puffed his way across the lobby.

"The mayor does not allow smoking in this part of the office, Detective Alfano," she said.

Seeing the look on Alfano's face, she immediately regretted the comment and went back to her typing until the intercom box sounded.

"His Honor will see you now."

"Big of him," was Alfano's muttered reply. He looked at the secretary and took one last puff and held up the half-smoked cigarette for her to see. She gave him a disgusted look, opened a lower drawer in her desk and took out a glass ashtray. As he crushed his butt, he said thanks. The door buzzed and swung open.

Standing near his great oak desk was Mayor Edward Kelly. Police Commissioner Hayden sat in a large leather chair and did not rise. Patrick Nash, political boss and puppet master, stood looking out the window.

"Damn, it's good to see you again, Detective. There's lots of craziness out there, even for a Sunday."

The mayor pointed with his cigar to a chair next to the commissioner. Alfano thought of the secretary and realized the rules were different in the mayor's office.

"Thank you, Mayor. I'm not sure I understand any of it either—yet."

What Alfano did understand was that this man was now inextricably involved in his life, both personally and professionally. Mayor Kelly hadn't a clue about what he had done or that the price had been Gini Gail's life, and even if he did, he wouldn't understand. Alfano thought most politicians were blind to the results of their actions.

"I understand that you were on the river last night when that motor launch exploded," the mayor said. "Why? Was it part of what we talked about a few days ago?"

"As I told you last week, I was doing my job and following up a tip," Alfano said. "The tip was that someone was going to sabotage the seaplanes. The only way to do that was on the water. I took a chance on the river."

"Lucky guess?" Hayden said.

"Sometimes luck is all you have, Commissioner."

Alfano turned back to the mayor.

"Does he know what this is all about?"

He nodded toward the commissioner.

"Yes, he knows what you told me," the mayor said. "As well as Mr. Nash."

Alfano had known that Kelly would tell Nash everything; Hayden was another matter, but not his problem.

"The fireboat captain thinks there were dozens of cans of gasoline onboard the runaway. They caught fire somehow and the boat exploded just past the Michigan Avenue Bridge. We could see the cans stacked in the stern when the boat went by. One man was driving it, were are not if there were others on board. Somewhere between the Wabash Bridge and Michigan Avenue he or they must have jumped off—or were killed when the boat exploded. Luckily, no one on the bridge was hurt or burned."

"Any idea who the pilot was?" Nash asked.

"We are working on a theory, but it's only that, a theory," Alfano said. "But we believe he was going out on the lake to attack General Balbo's planes."

"Just like you thought, Holy Mother of God," Kelly said. "And you stopped it."

"Hardly. From witness reports, it seems a woman was shooting at the boat as it headed upriver. We gather that she shot at the boat twice from bridges as the launch sped toward the lake. The witnesses say she was firing a pistol."

"A woman, a pistol?"

"Yes to both. She may be the same suspect who has murdered more than seven people during the last few weeks, both here in Chicago and in Milwaukee—brutally tortured them and then strangled them. No proof yet, but we are close to finding out who she is. Our hunch is that all the involved parties are related to the arrival of General Balbo. My sergeant thinks that it's politically motivated."

"Politics? You've got to be kidding me."

Alfano glanced toward Nash, still standing at the window.

"I never kid, sir. Yes, Italian politics, as in the fascists versus the communists. I'm leaning toward it myself," Alfano added.

"No one plays politics in my town," Nash said. "I mean our town."

"It's okay, Pat," the mayor said. "In a day or two, this will all blow over. Balbo and his Italian thugs will be gone."

Alfano stared at Kelly.

"You call this guy a thug? Look what he's doing for business in this city, your city. Hell, there were more than a hundred thousand people waiting for him on Navy Pier alone. And you call him a thug?"

"Sorry, bad choice of words. I don't have much sympathy for the fascists," Kelly said, with the ease of someone used to quickly backpedaling. "So you think this same woman strangled these people?"

"It's possible. We are chasing down some leads. One of the dead men, an Italian, went to school at Loyola. They may have more for me there."

Alfano looked at his watch.

"I'm running late," he told them.

Nash walked across the thick carpet to Alfano.

"Detective, you're doing a hell of a job out there, and we wish we had two dozen like you. Ten years ago the mob, then the Depression, and now all this with the fair and all—a hell of a job, thanks."

He put his hand out and shook Alfano's.

"There's a *but* somewhere in all this bullshit," Alfano said.

"Tsk, tsk, Alfano, your language," Hayden said.

"As if you have the tongue of a virgin, Commissioner," Alfano shot back.

"Stop it you two," Kelly admonished. "Detective, the real reason I've called you down here is to celebrate your recent success stopping the bombings on the day of the fair's opening in May. You are a real Chicago hero, and I'm proud of you and your men. You saved a lot of lives that day."

"And not to mention the opening of the Century of Progress Fair," Nash threw in.

The mayor added, "Yes, and that too. A grateful city thanks you, Detective."

Alfano eyed the three men. There was a fishy smell in the room. He'd already received a commendation and plaque that now lay on a chair in his apartment. That plaque and a dime would get you a cup of coffee. Why did he feel that a shoe was about to drop?

"Detective Alfano, this city needs heroes and you are one of our finest detectives and a credit to your people."

"My people?"

"Those in the Italian community, those who are celebrating General Balbo. Those who are working hard to make this city special," Kelly said. "Tomorrow night there is a celebration at the Congress Hotel to honor General Balbo and his crew. It's sponsored by the Sons of Italy; they are going to make him an honorary member."

"I thought Balbo was already an Italian," Alfano said, realizing that no one in the office understood the paradox of the honor. "I've also heard that you might name a street after him."

"In the works, Detective. Meanwhile, I have a special assignment for you. Tomorrow, I want you at the Congress Hotel to represent our great police department, and I want you at the head table with me, some of the aldermen, the Italian ambassador, and other guests. I want you sitting at my right hand."

Alfano looked at Kelly as if someone had told him that the Pope was an Irishman. After everything that had happened during the last twenty-four hours, all Alfano wanted now was four hours of sleep. Instead the mayor wanted him to sit all pretty-like at a fucking banquet.

"Too much to do. I can't, sir," he told the mayor.

"You have no choice in this. Consider it an order," Nash said, and then looked at the mayor.

"I don't give them too often, Detective," Kelly said. "Tomorrow night, I want you there with General Balbo and me. Jesus, Tony, do it for your home country. It's a goddamn honor I'm handing you."

Alfano looked at the men. The mayor's order sat like a brick in his stomach.

"I can't. No tuxedo and my formal uniform stinks of mothballs. Besides having a killer to catch, I've got nothing to wear."

Nash reached into his wallet and drew out a crisp one hundred dollar bill.

"See Jacob at Baskin's on State Street. He will set you up. In fact I've already called him. There's a tuxedo waiting for you as well as shoes. After all, Detective Alfano, you are Chicago's best plainclothes detective. You might as well be the best dressed."

"THE FUCKER ACTUALLY SAID THAT?" Sergeant McDunnah asked, when Alfano walked into the Racine Station. "I can see it all now. You will be known as the tuxedo detective."

"One more crack, Sergeant, and I'll make you go as my aide—in fact, you are going as my sidekick. We'll work it out somehow. I'll pick up the tux tomorrow morning, I don't have

to be there until eight-thirty. Maybe they can find you something to eat in the kitchen. We have a lot to do before then.
Any more on the boat or the driver?"

"People saw someone climb out of the Chicago River
near the Michigan Avenue Bridge minutes after the explosion.
Could be our guy, but we got nothing more to go on than normal height and normal size. Some said he had black hair. I also
have a report of a stolen boat from the Lincoln Park lagoon.
The owner lives in Racine and came down for the festivities.
When he went to his boat this morning, it was gone."

"Boat have a name?" Alfano asked.

"*Blackhawk*. The owner is a history buff and likes the old
Indian name. That fits with what I saw last night."

"You saw the name of the boat?"

"When it went roaring by on fire, like some Viking funeral
boat, I caught the name on the stern. I'm fairly certain it is, or
was, his boat."

"Anyone see who stole it or when?" Alfano asked.

"No. But according to the harbormaster, who was watching for boats coming and going near where the seaplanes were
to anchor, he saw the *Blackhawk* leave early Saturday morning.
He lost sight of her when she rounded the end of Navy Pier.
He never gave it a thought until the owner told him it'd gone
missing."

"Last night it was coming from up the river. My guess is
that whoever took it, loaded the gasoline there. There's a dozen
working docks and landings along that stretch of river south
of the Roosevelt Street Bridge. Send some patrol cars out there
to look around, maybe something will pop. In the morning I'm
going up to Loyola to talk to the admissions people. Maybe
they have more on this Donna Delucca or whatever the hell
her name is. Right now, I'm exhausted. I'm going home and
you go home too, Sergeant. Take your wife to noon Mass, have
a great dinner and get a good night's sleep. I have a feeling this
is not over."

29

ALFANO drove through the Loop to the North Side college campus. The admissions hall was in a ground-floor wing of the administration building.

A woman sat behind a counter, stacks of papers to her left and right. As Alfano watched, she took one paper from the left, looked down the page, made a check in the corner, then moved it to the right. He coughed.

"Oh, I'm sorry. Please excuse me. The monsignor has me looking through these papers, just a bit of bureaucracy. May I help you?"

Alfano introduced himself, showed his star, and then told her about his need to check on the whereabouts of any foreign students at the college. He was especially concerned about students from Italy and Rome.

"Oh, my, I certainly hope everything is okay. You are the second person in the last few weeks to ask the same question."

She told him about the woman claiming to be from the fair, looking for potential employees who could speak Italian.

"I was so busy that day, I allowed her to look at the list of graduate students. She spent an hour going over names, then left. I haven't heard anything since then."

"Did she leave a name, a phone number, address?"

"I made a note in my calendar. One moment, please."

Alfano waited as the woman pulled her thick day-to-day schedule out and opened it. "Let's see, somewhere around the middle of June. Yes, here it is. Donna Delucca is the name she gave. Pleasant woman, a touch severe, but then again women dress so strangely these days. I just don't know what's happening."

Alfano asked again if Delucca had given an address.

"No, but she did say she was with the staff at the Italian Pavilion. I made a note. Maybe she can be reached there."

Alfano thought for a moment, then asked, "Do you have a list of Italian exchange students? Any students who only just arrived this past winter from Italy?"

The secretary said yes, but that it would take a few minutes to research.

"Why don't you get a cup of coffee?" she suggested. "I'll need about fifteen minutes."

Alfano went for coffee. When he returned, the woman handed him a folded piece of paper. She smiled and then returned to her stacks of papers. Alfano exited the building and strolled through the campus. The summer, only days on, was now wide open. The Midwest heat and humidity had built up during the morning. His shirt, damp with sweat, stuck to his back. The faint smell of smoke and gasoline clung to the suit jacket he hadn't needed to bring.

The campus was quiet; summer recess was in full flight, and only a few students walked the grounds. He slung his jacket over his shoulder; more smoke odor squeezed out. He tipped his fedora back on his head, found a bench in the shade of large beech tree, and lit a cigarette before opening the piece of paper the administrator had handed him. Three names with addresses were on the list: Lucca Barone, Salvatore Rizzo, and Matteo Cavallo.

Now Matteo Cavallo is brutally dead. This was a hit, pure and simple. Shit, I've seen dozens of murder victims. Where do the DeAngelos fit in? Why them? Where are these other two, and, where the hell is this woman?

ALFANO left the Loyola campus, turned the Packard south on Lake Shore Boulevard and headed to the World's Fair. As he drove, the warm air pushed its way through the open car window. On his left, Lake Michigan was a blue mirror, not a ripple could be seen. One lone sailboat, its sail limp, drifted on the glass-like surface.

He'd not been back to the fairgrounds since opening day, the day his girlfriend killed herself with a bullet through her heart. There'd been no reason to go. All he remembered from that day was chaos, bombs, a man jumping to his death and the look on Gini's face. There'd been absolutely no reason to return—until now.

He held up his detective star at the gate and drove to the small parking area near the Italian Pavilion. Thousands of people jammed the esplanade while the Rocket Cars of the Sky Ride slowly coasted overhead. The Hall of Science stood majestically to his right as he entered; the Swedish and Czech exhibits were across the promenade. High above and beyond was the façade of Soldier Field. Alfano shivered.

He strolled into the Italian Pavilion, where a cute young woman in a peasant's costume stood in the center of the lobby, handing out leaflets and talking to the visitors. A square bandage was affixed to her cheek.

"Good afternoon"—Alfano squinted at her name-plate—"Maria. I'm Detective Alfano with the Chicago Police. Can you direct me to the pavilion's offices?"

He held up his star.

Maria blanched and started to visibly shake.

"Are you all right? " Alfano asked, and took her arm. "Do

you need to sit?"

"I'm not allowed to sit. Just give me a moment."

She took in a breath.

"It's the heat. Even with the cooling system, I get flushed. I'm sorry, Detective . . . ?"

"Alfano. Just point me to the offices, and I'll let you get back to your job."

"Through that hallway and keep going. The signs will point the way."

Alfano looked at the girl again.

"Are you all right, Miss DeRosa? Should I call someone?"

"No, my supervisor, Miss Nardo, is watching us right now. No, I'll be fine. But thank you. Please take one of these brochures; that will take her mind off me for a while."

Alfano accepted the pamphlet and glanced at the image of Balbo's seaplanes on the cover.

"Very exciting, isn't it, all the festivities? Did you get a chance to meet General Balbo?"

Again Maria paled.

She stuttered, "No, unfortunately, I was at my parents' restaurant, so I missed him."

She took another deep breath.

"It would have been exciting," she said.

"To say the least, you take care of yourself. And thank you for the directions."

Alfano walked partway down the hallway Maria had indicated. His more than twenty years of reading people told him that she was afraid—afraid of him or something she knew. He stopped and walked back to her. Her back was to him.

"Excuse me again. I'm sorry."

She dropped the brochures on the floor. They scattered in every direction. Hands shaking, she started to gather them up. Miss Nardo, or so Alfano guessed, hurried over and began to help. The supervisor started to say something to the girl; Alfano interrupted her.

"I'm sorry, ma'am. I'm Detective Alfano with the Chicago Police and this woman is being very helpful in an investigation I'm involved with."

He flashed his star.

"She was giving me directions to your offices. I startled her. It is completely my fault. With your permission, may I ask her a few more questions?"

The woman looked sternly at Maria then at Alfano.

"Well, I guess so. Just don't take too much of her time or I'll have to dock her pay. Maria, why don't you and the detective go to the break room, but be back here in ten minutes."

"Yes, ma'am."

"Lead the way, Miss DeRosa," Alfano said.

The break room, in contrast to the pavilion, was severe, with steel chairs and hard metal tables arranged around the small room. Alfano heard a faint echo when he spoke.

"Sit, please," he said. "I hope I don't get you into trouble with that woman. She's a pistol, isn't she?"

Maria slowly nodded in affirmation, but her eyes were wide and unblinking.

"I really didn't mean to put you on the spot out there. I just had a question, and I thought you might have the answer."

"Detective Alfano, I need this job, I really do. Miss Nardo will fire me on the spot if I'm not back when she said. She's already been a bit nasty to me."

"Now why is that?"

"I was late this morning, and she had to hand out the brochures. You can bet she took me to task for being tardy. Now your questions only make this worse. I need to get back."

She started to stand.

"Just a few questions, then you can get back."

He took out his notebook.

"Do you know a woman by the name of Donna Delucca?"

30

MARIA DEROSA took a shaky breath and again blanched. Her perfectly applied make-up couldn't hide the fear in her expression. She put her palms together and slowly rubbed them together.

"No," she whispered in answer to his question, her eyes downcast.

Alfano made a show of writing a note in his book, then spoke gently but firmly.

"Miss DeRosa, I've been doing this a long time and I can tell when someone is avoiding the truth. Everything about you says that you are afraid of me for some reason and that you *do* know this Donna Delucca. Now I understand why you are afraid of me—after all, I'm a real tough guy and cop."

He smiled, and Maria relaxed a bit when she looked up and saw his expression.

"But when I mentioned Delucca, there was more than acknowledgment. I saw fear. Why is that?"

There was a pitcher of water on the counter. Alfano poured each of them a glass. He offered her the glass, and she sipped.

"Please tell me what you know about this Delucca woman," he said.

"She's very scary," Maria confessed, looking as if she might bolt out of the room.

He smiled at her again and she continued.

"She stopped me in the lobby a few weeks ago and asked, like you, where the office was. I told her. Then she introduced herself and, for some reason, touched my cheek. It was strange, but it scared the devil out me. I assumed she was with the staff of the pavilion and the fair. But she scared me."

"Assumed? There's more," Alfano said. "You were afraid as soon as I introduced myself. Why is that?"

She went back to rubbing her hands together, glanced nervously about the room. Finally, she said, "I thought you were here about last night."

"What about last night? What happened last night?"

DeRosa stopped fidgeting and looked at Alfano.

"The boat, the shooting, the explosion."

"What shooting?"

DeRosa looked confused, eyebrows furrowed.

"You're not here to ask me about the shooting down at the river?" she said.

Now it was Alfano's turn to be puzzled. He thought for a long moment, then took out a cigarette and offered one to Maria.

"Now what do you know about last night on the river? Is that where you got that cut on your cheek?" he asked her.

She put her hand to her cheek as if belatedly trying to hide the wound.

"That woman, that Donna Delucca—she tried to kill us. She shot at us. A splinter hit me in the face."

"Now why would she do that?"

He had to wait for an answer, but eventually she seemed to reach a decision and said simply, "She was trying to stop my boyfriend and his friend from blowing up the seaplanes."

"How could she do that?" Alfano asked, keeping his voice even.

"She was shooting at us from the bridge over the river.

When Sal left with the boat, she went after him. You must protect us from her. She'll kill us. Kill us all—like she did Matteo."

"Matteo? Matteo Cavallo?"

"Yes, we found out he was murdered, probably by her."

"Who is this Sal?" Alfano asked, thinking that he already had a pretty good idea from the names on the Loyola list.

"A friend of my boyfriend, Lucca Barone. They came here from Rome to go to Loyola."

"Names, again?"

Alfano touched the tip of the pencil to his tongue. Now they were getting somewhere.

"Sal Rizzo and Lucca Barone—but Lucca wouldn't have anything to do with Sal after their friend was killed."

"Matteo Cavallo?"

"Yes, Matteo. He came with them from Italy. Sal told us he was murdered. He found the body. That's when I told Lucca we had to get away."

Alfano's mind was racing. *The recently discovered Cavallo, the woman's phone call, the river, the boat exploding, Balbo's seaplanes, the two black victims, Bova, a length of silk rope, and the wet body of Mary Ann DeAngelo—the hideous wreckage of one crazed woman's amusements.*

"You said this woman was headed to the pavilion offices when you first met her. Do you know if she did go to the offices?"

"Yes, about an hour later I was headed here on a break, and I saw her leave the office and head out the rear door."

"You think she knows someone there?"

"Maybe—she was there a long time."

A sharp tap on the door interrupted the interrogation. Maria broke down into tears as Miss Nardo marched in.

"Please leave now, I'm conducting an investigation," Alfano barked.

Nardo looked at DeRosa. Her intention had been to fire

the girl. Seeing her in tears, she hesitated.

"What—?" she started to ask.

"Out, now. Goddamn it!" Alfano said.

Nardo quickly spun back to the door and closed it behind her.

"Thank you, I need this job," Maria said with a sob. "That's why I'm here even after all that has happened. If I miss one day I'll lose everything, and we need the money."

"You knew Matteo Cavallo?" Alfano said to Maria. "You knew he was dead?"

She nodded her head, still crying.

"Yes, Sal said so."

Alfano crushed his cigarette into an ashtray on the table. He took the still-lit one from Maria's limp fingers and crushed it too.

"Rizzo and Barone are in trouble, I can tell you that. Who was on the boat? Was it Rizzo?"

"Yes."

"Is he still alive?"

"Yes, he jumped off before the explosion. I saw him this morning before I came to work. They are both okay."

"Where are they?"

She gave him the address of Lucca's apartment off Taylor. It matched the address on the Loyola paperwork for Barone; most likely, Rizzo and Barone would stay put for the moment. Meanwhile, Alfano wanted this woman, this murderer. He wanted Donna Delucca.

HE called McDunnah from a pay phone in the hallway and brought him up to speed on Maria DeRosa's revelations.

"And send me a couple of patrolmen to retrieve Miss DeRosa," he said. "She's a material witness; hold her on that. I'll be back to the station in an hour."

Alfano waited with Maria until the two patrolmen arrived.

"You Detective Alfano?" one of them asked.

"Yes, and don't do anything other than get this woman to the Racine Street Station. See Sergeant McDunnah. If she's not there in ten minutes, I'll personally write the both of you up."

The four left the break room and headed toward the pavilion's entry. Sandwiched between the two uniformed cops, Maria walked slowly, certain a thousand eyes were on her. She nervously scanned the crowd; sure that someone from the neighborhood would spot her. Her parents would be furious. She wiped her eyes; they stung as she tried to hold back the sobs that had begun in the breakroom.

"There," she said suddenly to Alfano and pointed. "That's Delucca."

Standing out from the mass of visitors that filled the large entrance hall, a tall woman purposely wove her way through the crowd.

"You," Alfano jerked his thumb at one of the patrolmen, "get her to the station. Tell Sergeant McDunnah I have a lead on the killer and I'll call him when I can. You," he pointed at the other officer, "are with me."

Alfano's eyes never left Delucca, who seemed overly concerned about the people in her way. She never looked around.

With the patrolman trailing him several paces behind, Alfano stayed to the edge of the mass of people crowded in the atrium. He watched Delucca head toward a pair of doors; a sign to one side read *Pavilion Offices*. A security guard stood at idle attention near the doors. Delucca said something to the man and waved a paper in front of his face. He quickly opened one of the doors.

After working his way through the crush of fairgoers, Alfano flashed his star at the guard.

"The woman who was just here, do you know her?"

"No, sir, but then again I'm new here."

"What was that she showed you?" Alfano asked.

"A pass issued by someone from the Italian consulate," he answered. "Was official, I'm sure. With that aviator and his people all about, we were briefed on the correct passes that have been issued. Be glad when they leave, just too much craziness if you ask me. She was kind of agitated though," he added.

"Where did you send Delucca? What office?"

"Delucca? Weren't her name on the pass. Name on the pass was Acerbi, Carla Acerbi."

Alfano headed down the hallway toward the offices; the main office was around the corner on the left side, the guard said. Alfano assumed that's where the woman would be.

When he turned the corner, she was, standing halfway down the corridor yelling at a short, wiry man in a linen suit and buff-colored straw boater. The argument was heated.

"You stay here," Alfano said to the patrolman and then turned to the pair. "Miss Acerbi, could I have a moment?" he shouted.

As Alfano rushed toward the pair, Acerbi shoved the man hard against the wall and dashed down the hallway. The small man slumped to the floor. In ten strides, Acerbi reached the door and yanked it open. She was briefly silhouetted in the bright sun streaming through the opening, before she bolted through the door, slamming it shut behind her.

Alfano ran past the man on the floor and followed Acerbi out the door. In the brilliant sunlight he instantly realized that his chances of catching her were gone. Ten thousand patrons filled the walks and promenade. She had slipped into the crowd and been carried away by the mass of visitors, as if she had dove into a fast river and the current had swept her away. Alfano swore and turned back to the man in the hallway, who was being helped to his feet by the patrolman.

"Who the hell are you? You are not supposed to be here,"

the man said to Alfano.

Alfano pushed his star into the man's face.

"Who the hell is she?"

"Who?"

"Don't fuck with me. Who is that woman? She work for you?"

"She was asking for help. She was confused."

"Right," said Alfano. "Who are you?"

"Guido Barbieri. I work here."

"And the woman? Who is she?" Alfano asked again.

The man retrieved his boater from the concrete floor.

"I don't know her, never saw her before," he insisted. "If you'll excuse me, I have work to do."

Barbieri moved as if to leave.

"Not a chance, you're coming with me."

The small man smiled.

"Let me save you some agony, Detective. I'm a member of the Italian consulate with diplomatic immunities. We are the visitors you don't fuck with."

"Cute, nice, real cute. I really don't care. Turn around."

"What the hell?"

Alfano grabbed the man and spun him around, then slammed him against the wall. At the same time, he wrenched the man's right arm up and high. Barbieri screamed.

"Resisting arrest, are we? Not good," Alfano said, pushing the man's arm even higher.

Barbieri screamed from the pain.

The patrolman stood back and watched. If he was shocked, he wisely kept it to himself as Alfano kicked Barbieri's legs apart, pulled out his handcuffs and hooked the man up.

"You may have diplomatic immunity," Alfano whispered in the small man's ear. "But none of that works if no one knows where you are."

31

THE PATROLMAN and Alfano walked Barbieri out of the pavilion to Alfano's car where he was loaded in the back. Alfano dropped them off at the station.

"Tell the sergeant I'll be back in an hour. That son of bitch will complain to high heaven," he pointed to Barbieri, "Sergeant McDunnah will know how to handle him. Tell him I have to pick up something downtown."

"Yes sir," the cop said as he pushed Barbieri ahead of him toward the station entry. He shook his head in wonder as Alfano pulled away from the curb.

"What did you do with the girl?" Alfano asked two hours later when he finally returned to the Racine Street Station.

McDunnah watched as Alfano draped a bag containing his new tuxedo over the back of his chair and place a box holding patent leather shoes on the desk.

"She's gone home," the sergeant said. "We know where to find her. I actually know her parents and their restaurant. Damn fine place, Pompeii's Grotto—you know it. We've eaten there a few times. From the reaction I got from her father, she's in a load of trouble. Hell, he's better than any judicial system. I wouldn't worry about her; she's on ice until we need her."

"Barbieri?"

"Different horse, different color. Now that 'diplomat' is a piece of work. It took all of two phone calls, and within the hour the FBI was visiting. I gladly handed the man over. Seems the feds have been watching the guy. They want to encourage him to return home, even if they have to march him to the ship in handcuffs. His spying days are over."

"By the by, that rookie you had in tow was over the top about you. What did you do, Detective? Go all Keystone cop on Barbieri?

"This Carla Acerbi?" Alfano asked, trying to change the conversation.

"We got nothing so far. Bubkes—nothing from the feds or Washington either. Maybe this Barbieri guy knows, but he wasn't talking. The immunity thing trumps all."

"Shit. Based on DeRosa's statement, Acerbi has to be the killer," Alfano said.

"Yes, and it was Acerbi who tried to stop the boat and Sal Rizzo. What the hell does that mean?"

"I think it means that someone wanted these boys dead *before* they could attack the seaplanes. Only one person would want that. Think about it. The embarrassment would be very real and right now Il Duce can't afford to let that happen. Considering what's going on in Italy, my guess is that Delucca, a.k.a. Acerbi, is working for the fascists. She is here to stop them, and from the look of the results of Saturday she may have succeeded. Acerbi's connections to people at the fair, especially this Barbieri, certainly bear that out."

"Makes some sense in a bizarre way," McDunnah said as he wrote the name Carla Acerbi on a slip of paper and stuck it under the crude sketch he had posted earlier in the week.

"Anything on the license plate the kids saw?"

"Still looking, maybe later today. So nothing there, yet."

"She has to be holed up somewhere, have one of the other detectives check and see if the Italians own or have other apartments in the city. A long shot, but she might be in one of them."

Two hours later their search proved fruitless. If there were a secret apartment of even an Oldsmobile owned by the Italian government in Chicago, it didn't show up on any records. They both agreed that it could be under the name of a private citizen or even a business. It would take a lot more digging.

"And what are you going to do about it tonight?" McDunnah asked.

"Nothing, Sergeant, nothing. I'm to attend the dinner at the insistence of the mayor and Nash. This monkey suit is a result of their caring so much about little old me."

Alfano showered and dressed in the station's locker room. When he walked out into the detectives bull pit, there was stunned silence.

"If any of you say a thing . . ." Alfano threatened.

McDunnah smiled and simply announced, "Ladies and gentlemen, may I introduce to you our head waiter for tonight, Detective Anthony Alfano."

A smattering of laughs and applause rose from the other detectives and patrolmen.

McDunnah slowed and drove past the massive Michigan Avenue façade of the Congress Hotel. A dozen taxis and limousines sat bumper to bumper on the broad boulevard that separated the hotel from Grant Park and Buckingham Fountain.

"Swing around to the Harrison Street side," Alfano said to McDunnah. They parked the car next to the curb. After Alfano exited the car, he straightened his tux and leaned back through the window. "Find someplace to park this thing—and make it near. I want to be out of here as soon as the niceties are done."

"I never thought you could look this good, Detective. The tuxedo hangs just right—gives you some swagger. I suggest though that you keep the jacket buttoned; open, I can see the strap to your shoulder holster and the butt of your revolver."

There was a tap on the hood of the car. Both men looked up and saw one of McDunnah's patrolmen staring through the windshield.

"What do you want, McGuire?" Alfano said to the cop.

The patrolman looked twice at Alfano, who was buttoning his double-breasted jacket.

"Jesus, Detective. I's didn't sees it was you. You look so different. I mean you look good, but . . ." He looked through the car's windshield. "And is that the Sergeant? Holy Mary, Mother of God."

McGuire looked again at the frowning face of his sergeant, put up his hands in surrender, and turned away like nothing had happened.

"I'll be out here for now, if I need anything I'll send Mc-Guire," McDunnah said. "He's a good kid. After the guests arrive I'll move into the lobby. Just don't forget about me, okay, Detective? Remember, I know where the car is."

Alfano entered on the Harrison Street side and walked into the hotel's rich, over-decorated lobby. The place had a glorious and jaded past. Less than ten years earlier, Alfano had come here with a warrant to arrest Al Capone in his eighth-floor suite. The information had been bad, and Capone wasn't in when Alfano went knocking on the door. However he did spend some time wandering through the lavish suite with two of Capone's thugs watching his every move. Over the years, he'd had a drink or two in some of the quieter corners of the hotel's unofficial bars as well as some less-than-elegant encounters with overly drunk aldermen. In addition, somewhere upstairs was the suite occasionally occupied by the recently assassinated Mayor Cermak. Tony smiled to himself, remembering a West Side alderman and the very cute, very mature-looking, but very underage girl from Indiana shacked up in the politician's room. Yeah, sometimes even the bad guys threw a seven.

The characteristic sounds of an Italian band drifted through the lobby from someplace above Alfano. Signs were posted discreetly, directing guests of the party to the upper floors and the Gold Room, where the main celebration would take place. Alfano glanced at his watch; thirty minutes until the guests of honor were to arrive.

"Already checking to see if it's time to go, Detective?"

Alfano gritted his teeth at the sight of the puppet master.

"Nash," he said grudgingly.

"They are running a little late, but no need to worry," said Nash.

He looked Alfano up and down.

"I also see that my hundred accomplished a lot. I do have to say, you look good."

Alfano tried to stretch his shirt collar with his finger.

"Thankfully, this doesn't require tails for us common folk," he said to Nash. "That cutaway on you looks pretty damn good—for a public servant."

"I do my best for the city and its people."

Alfano pulled out a cigarette and lit it. Nash waved to someone and quickly left.

Alfano had heard stories about Nash and Mayor Cermak. It was hard to believe it had been four months since Cermak's death at the hand of an Italian assassin. But it wasn't hard to believe the stories of political deals and shenanigans, ending up with Mayor Edward Kelly as mayor. Much as he disliked rumors, Alfano didn't discount them in this case.

McDunnah arrived. Alfano watched the sergeant cross the lobby with his poker face on.

"Where did you park the car?" he asked, when McDunnah drew near.

"I put McGuire in charge of the damn thing. It's parked around the corner, on Harrison. So, Detective, what now?"

"Cool our heels until this thing starts, smile nice, shake

hands, pretend we're having a great time, then leave."

"I like it."

More guests arrived, filling the lush lobby and meandering toward the elevators and stairway. Alfano heard Italian as well as English. It was obvious that many of the men had rented their formal wear, whereas the women had splurged on gowns and jewelry. As for the headgear some of the ladies had donned—calling them hats would have stretched the definition of the word. Most looked as if they'd been stolen from a birdcage or plucked from the ass of a peacock.

32

CARLA ACERBI slid her car into a parking spot three blocks away from the Congress Hotel. The iron stairs that lead to the 'L' clattering above were to her left as she walked down Van Buren Street. She'd spent part of the morning looking for the best location to manage an escape. She wanted options; the 'L' was one of them. She placed a large sign on the dashboard that read ITALIAN EMBASSY — OFFICIAL BUSINESS, then checked the Luger and extra clip she carried in a large black patent leather clutch. If she needed more firepower than that, it wouldn't matter; she'd already be dead. The invitation for the evening's event was folded next to the pistol. She checked her make-up in the rearview mirror. There were at least three hours of sunlight left. Everything in order, she placed a thin wrap over her shoulders that complemented the dark green dress she wore, locked the car and began to walk toward Wabash Avenue. Under the iron girders of the elevated railroad, sketchy men stood in small groups. A few leaned against the dirty walls of the buildings. The men watched her lasciviously. She ignored them until one became too persistent: "Come on, doll, where you going? Herman here knows what you's want. Herman knows what every doll wants."

Acerbi turned and looked at the man. Thin to gaunt, three-day stubble of beard, a suit she was sure she could smell from fifty feet, a rope to hold up his pants, and a very smart mouth. She strolled up to him. His friends, standing next to him, shrank back.

"There is absolutely nothing you have that I would want," she said. "But I have something for you."

"Me? What, I have . . ."

He looked into her eyes.

"What the fuck?"

Acerbi jammed her knee into his crotch and drove her palm into the underside of his jaw. The man's eyes bulged. He dropped to his knees and rolled to one side, clutching his groin.

"Goddamn, lady, you didn't need to do that to Herman," one of the other men said. "Shit, why the hell did you do that?"

Acerbi stared at Herman's friend until he instinctively stepped back. It was the eyes, the woman's eyes—they looked dead, lifeless. Herman's buddy put his hands up in surrender.

"Tell him, next time, to watch his mouth," Acerbi told them.

She strolled past the Congress Hotel, crossed Michigan Avenue and walked into Grant Park that bordered one of Chicago's most famous streets. There she found a front-row bench where she could watch the hotel and the hundreds of guests arriving for the Son's of Italy celebration of General Italo Balbo.

How fitting that the man should die amongst his people.

HOW the cop had found her in the hallway with Barbieri still puzzled Acerbi. Her meeting with the little bastard had not gone well. Once Salvatore Rizzo and his crew had been stopped, she'd expected to leave Chicago. Before going to meet Barbieri, she had packed and purchased train tickets; her suitcases were in the trunk of her car. Her plan was to take the Illinois Central streamliner to New Orleans then book a cabin on a local steamer to South America. Her goal was Buenos Aires, Argentina. She would then quietly send for her family.

Instead, the diminutive fascist agent had sat behind his desk, looking smug at delivering a new assignment.

"You did a magnificent job in stopping these communists from embarrassing the government," he'd said. "We have others looking for his comrades, not that I care about them. Maybe they will be found, maybe not. Our concern is the reputation of the Italian government here in America. My communications with Rome confirm their appreciation for your work."

"Thank you. The fools made it easy. Now I am looking forward to returning home to Italy."

"You are taking the train to New York as your exit point?"

"Yes, tomorrow," she lied.

The agent steepled his fingers beneath his chin.

"You are not done. I have new orders for you from Rome."

He slid an envelope across the desk.

Acerbi resisted the urge to reach across the desk and grab him by the throat, annoyed as much at being delayed leaving as having to receive instructions of any kind from Barbieri.

"And these are?" she asked tightly.

"The envelope contains the necessary maps, schedules and directives you need to proceed to your next operation. I have been told you are very thorough and require precise approvals for your . . . activities. You will find them there. Please destroy the envelope after this meeting."

"And these orders are?"

"It is evident that the Prime Minister is concerned about all this popularity for his second-in-command. While he is, of course, very pleased with the accomplishments of the general, he is quite upset that there has not been significant praise and adulation of himself and of his government. After all, the

Minister and Rome have worked for many years to celebrate the accomplishments and contributions of Italy to the American's World's Fair. Unfortunately, here in Chicago, it seems to be all about General Balbo."

"The Americans love heroes. Look at Lindbergh and their new president," she said. "Il Duce is jealous of Balbo? I find that hard to believe."

"Jealous is not the word I would use. It is more . . . concern."

"This will all blow over when the general returns home in triumph. The Italians are very proud of their hero and deservedly so."

"You see, Miss Acerbi, there is the problem. Once the general and his squadron return home, it will be difficult to control their comments and interviews. The government can only do so much to manage these heroes—and they *will* be hailed as heroes."

"Get to the point," Acerbi said. "What is my role in this little play that you are concocting?"

"Our government will not allow someone to appropriate more power than it is willing to give."

"Even if that man is the government's second-in-command?"

"Yes, there are no exceptions."

"This is foolish. What can possibly be gained?"

"That is not your concern nor mine. We are soldiers, and we follow orders."

"And that order is what?"

"General Balbo is not to return to Italy—alive."

Acerbi stared at the man.

"You want me to kill him?"

"Of course," Barbieri said. "We cannot allow this acclaim to grow."

"Fuck the acclaim. I'm done. I did my part."

She stood and headed for the door.

"Tell the assholes, I'm done," she said.

He followed her to the hallway.

"After this evening—then you are done," he said.

"I refuse."

Barbieri reached into his suit coat and extracted another envelope. He held it out to her.

"Look at this, then decide, though I'm sure it will no longer be a problem."

Acerbi glared at the man and took the envelope. It contained a single sheet of paper and a photo. After a glance, she refolded the paper and slipped it into the same pocket in which she'd placed the first envelope.

"If you or your people harm one hair on the head of my father, you will find that there is no place in the world you can hide. You know me, Barbieri. You know that what I'm saying is true."

In one smooth movement, she took hold of his collar and twisted the fabric.

"I mean it. In fact, I would enjoy cutting your throat. Yes, I think I would enjoy it very much."

She shoved him away hard enough that his head hit the wall knocking off his hat and he slumped downward; simultaneously, she half turned at the sounds of footsteps in the hallway. Someone yelled out her name—Acerbi. Wondering who, besides Barbieri, recognized her unnerved her momentarily. She glanced down at Barbieri, who glared up at her as her name again echoed through the hallway, then she turned and ran to the one door in the opposite direction of her unknown pursuer.

It had taken four hours to make it back to her apartment, four hours to make sure she wasn't tailed. Four hours to decide to carry out the new mission, after which she'd make sure that Barbieri had an accident—one he'd not recover from.

33

TWENTY MINUTES before the time noted on the invitation, Acerbi crossed Michigan Avenue and joined the hundreds of people jammed at the hotel entry. For the first time since leaving Rome, she heard many Italian words filling the air. The crowd provided cover but would also make assassinating the general exceedingly difficult. She needed to be within three meters of the man to be guaranteed a killing shot. In the chaos after the shot, she would escape with the rest of the terrified supporters. Barbieri's envelope held everything: tonight's schedule, her invitation, diagrams of the hotel's famous Gold Room, who would be sitting where, and train tickets. Train tickets she would not be using. All she needed to leave the city was in the trunk of her car. After tonight, she would disappear.

At the corner of Harrison and South Michigan Avenue, a policeman exited a large automobile, sergeant's stripes on his sleeve. Another cop jogged to a stop in front of the sergeant. As she passed the two men, she watched the sergeant hand the car keys to the other cop, a patrolman most likely.

The sergeant took a look at the striking woman, smiled and said, "Good evening, ma'am."

"Officer," she answered politely, before continuing to the front portico of the hotel.

ALFANO walked into the Gold Room. Its gilded walls arched to a lavishly coffered ceiling that extended over the surrounding mezzanine, reminding Alfano of churches he'd seen in Italy. More than a dozen golden electric wall sconces lit the room. Adorning the ceiling, trompe l'oeil paintings of cherubs, scantily clad women and muscular gods seemed to look down on the festivities. Spread across the rich carpeting were more than forty round tables, populated with flowers and glassware. There was no dance floor for this celebration. Waiters passed through the crowd, carrying trays of champagne glasses and canapés. Like Alfano, the other guests gaped in awe as they entered. Most had never been in this Americanized version of an Italian folly.

A group of the aviators who had flown in with Balbo stood together in a far corner of the room, answering questions, shaking hands with the men, and smiling at the heavily made-up women.

A lady approached Alfano, clipboard in hand.

"Detective Alfano, Bridgett Lorenzo. I'm with the organizing committee. You were pointed out to me by Mr. Nash— there by the door. And you look very handsome this evening in your tuxedo."

"Thank you, Miss Lorenzo, if you only knew," Alfano answered, and admired what he saw: dark eyes and hair, a natural luster to her rich olive complexion, warm smile. It also didn't hurt that she filled out the dark red gown she wore exceptionally well.

"Can I help you?" he asked her.

"I'm here to help *you*. Your place is four seats to the left from the center chair."

She pointed to the long banquet table at one end of the room.

"You will be sitting next to the mayor."

"The son of a bitch pulled it off," Alfano said softly."

"Sir?"

"Nothing, Miss Lorenzo, nothing. What am I to do while I sit there?"

"Other than enjoy the evening, nothing. There may be an acknowledgment of you by the mayor. As he introduces you, just stand and bow slightly, that's all."

"Good, I hate speeches."

She laughed.

"Not a big fan myself."

"When should I sit? I'd look awfully foolish up there right now."

"When the general and the mayor arrive, along with the leaders of the Italian community, just move toward them and hang to the edges. I expect that the mayor or someone will introduce you, then just stay nearby. When they move to the table, just follow. Not much more than that."

"No receiving line?"

"The schedule is too tight, unfortunately. I'm sure many of these people would love to meet the general—my mother certainly would. She's over there."

Miss Lorenzo pointed to a cluster of women talking.

"I think she's in love with General Balbo," she said, sotto-voce.

"He is a good looking guy, aristocratic bearing. Too bad he's a fascist."

"That doesn't bother my mother, but then again, she is from the old country," she said with a smile.

A mild commotion at the large double entry doors signaled the arrival of the honored guest.

"They are here. If you will excuse me, Detective."

Alfano watched Bridgett Lorenzo walk quickly toward the entry. He wished he were twenty years younger, or she was twenty years older. Either way would have worked.

A tight group of about a dozen men entered the room.

With them came the famous General Italo Balbo, smiling graciously. Wearing an elegant white officer's uniform, he stood taller than most of the crowd around him. To his right was a beaming Mayor Kelly. Alfano recognized many of the others in the group from various Italian organizations: the Knights of Columbus, the Sons of Italy, and one or two that under other circumstances would be on his arrest and charge list. He mentally shrugged. Tonight was a night of celebrations and festivities, and he had a free ticket. He might as well enjoy himself.

ACERBI had stepped into the crowded women's room to await the arrival of her target. She now joined the guests, standing shoulder to shoulder, as they waited in the lobby. Tonight she needed the cover the crowd provided. However, as usual, the unpredictability of a large group put her on edge. The pushing mass of excited partygoers could just as easily turn into a panicked mob or worse. She sensed the excitement growing in the room as people jostled for a view of the celebrated general.

If the goal were to kill the target with no regard for one's own safety or escape, any sociopath could do the job. In that case, the goal was to make a point, to kill, to be a martyr, not escape. Acerbi, on the other hand, had every reason to escape. She did not intend to die over this man or any man. They were all fools and only thought of themselves. For her, Balbo was now just a target; there was no emotional connection, none. There had been none with the others and there was none now.

She felt the advantage of no one suspecting a woman assassin and was counting on joining the swarm of people who would gather tightly around the general. At the precise moment, she would raise her pistol, fire, drop the weapon, and run with the rest of the fleeing and screaming throng. There would be no second chance. She moved with the crowd into the Gold Room.

Alfano smiled at a passing waiter, who skillfully balanced a tray of champagne glasses. The detective took one and then a sip. He watched the mayor shake hands with everyone while at the same time encouraging the general to move along further into the room.

"Politicians," Alfano mumbled, as much out of habit as annoyance.

He took another sip from his glass.

The crowd now converged toward Balbo. Men and women, young and old and—for tonight—the rich and poor. Some of the men wore tuxedos that had last seen the light when the wearer was married; others wore them casually and comfortably—taken together, it was a strange mix. The mayor had wanted a broad cross-section of Italian Chicagoans at the event, and even though His Honor was as Irish as a Dublin whore, he'd gotten his wish.

Alfano worked his way through the tide of guests, getting in position to join the higher-ups at the head table when appropriate. His eyes scanned the room and automatically caught the one thing he'd been trained to notice: a thing that didn't fit. In this case, it was a woman, taller and more arresting than the norm of matronly *signora*, slowly and methodically elbowing her way through the guests toward Balbo. She stopped halfway, maybe fifty feet from the general, and removed an item from her purse. She then slipped the patent leather clutch under her left arm, while her right hand deftly went to her side, hiding whatever she held in the lush folds of her gown. She was striking in a way that most women tried not to be. Even dressed as elegantly as she was, there was a decided lack of femininity about her. Not that she wasn't a woman; Alfano was sure that every inch of her was that. The difference was more in how she carried herself. When she turned and faced the mayor's entourage, Alfano gently set his glass of champagne on a table and drew out his weapon. He walked briskly toward the woman, weaving in and among the tables and chairs, his revolver hard to his side. When he was twenty feet away, she turned and stared carefully at him. Alfano saw recognition burst into her eyes; he tightened the grip on his gun, waiting for the inevitable. Suddenly, she spun on her heels and quickly headed back toward the door, pushing guests out of her way. Alfano had to jog to catch up to the fleeing woman.

"Miss Acerbi, we need to talk!" he yelled, as she headed down the stairs to the lobby. He followed in her wake, hindered by the mass of people trying to move in the opposite direction on the stairs. From midway down the stairs, he watched her quick-walk across the lobby and disappear around a corner. He looked around for McDunnah; the sergeant was in the lobby and they spotted each other at the same time. Alfano pointed to the hotel doors. McDunnah shot him a questioning look.

"Acerbi was in the ballroom and scrammed when she saw me," Alfano said, when the two men reached each other. "She's armed with a pistol."

He pointed toward the doors again.

"Balbo or the mayor?" McDunnah asked, as he and Alfano crossed the lobby.

"She was after Balbo I'm sure."

They reached the lobby doors.

"She's only seconds ahead of us. You go right, I'll go left," Alfano said.

Both on foot, they split. Alfano headed down Michigan Avenue to Congress Parkway. McDunnah turned south and went toward Harrison Street. As Alfano turned the corner onto Congress, he spotted her. She was running, her gown billowing around her legs; she stumbled but did not fall. She glanced back over her shoulder. Upon seeing Alfano, she expertly raised her pistol and fired. The bullet whizzed past his ear. He slammed himself into a shallow alcove in the stone face of the hotel. When he took a quick peek, another bullet took out a chunk of limestone. He caught stone fragments in his face.

"Shit," was all he could muster.

He looked again in time to see her round the corner at Wabash and disappear. Hugging the side of the building, he jogged to the corner, stopped, and took a quick peek. She was halfway down the block, looking for a gap in the stream of cars where she could cross to the other side. She looked back and fired again; this time the bullet shattered the plate glass window he was standing next to.

"Bitch," Alfano muttered.

Acerbi was pissed. Why had that cop been in the room? Ten seconds later it would have been over. Now it was all seriously fucked up. She looked left and right for an opening between the moving cars. Her first thought was to get back to her car; plan B was a taxi or something to get her as much separation from her pursuer as she could. Stealing a moving car was an idea, but the traffic jam would stop her in a block. She heard the rattling sound of the elevated train overhead.

"Maybe?" she thought, "just maybe."

She studied the overhead rails; they led to where she'd parked.

McDunnah, with the young patrolman McGuire now trailing him, ran down Harrison Street toward Wabash Avenue. Rounding the corner at full gallop, he almost knocked down the woman he'd seen not fifteen minutes earlier. He heard Alfano yell.

"It's her! She's got a gun."

McDunnah looked at the woman at the same instant she raised her weapon and fired. The shot zipped by his ear, but he heard a sickening cry from McGuire. There was another shot, and McDunnah tensed, thinking that this was it, but she was firing at Alfano, who'd broken cover when he saw McGuire go down. McDunnah watched Tony stumble and fall to the sidewalk.

The woman didn't look back. She bolted into the traffic and wove her way amongst the honking cars. Once on the other side, she ran north on Wabash.

Alfano clambered to his feet, swearing this was the last time he would ever wear new leather dress shoes to a fucking gunfight. He watched Acerbi, or whatever her real name was, running on the far side of the street.

"You okay, McDunnah?" he screamed over the roar of the train that screeched through the curve directly over them.

"Yes, but McGuire's down."

McDunnah knelt next to the young man. Even his time in the army during the war had not hardened the sergeant to the carnage of an arterial shot in the neck. Blood was everywhere. McGuire was dead.

"Find her, Tony. Kill the bitch," McDunnah said, holding the young man. "Get her."

Alfano turned and watched the green dress appear under the glare of a streetlight then disappear. He paralleled her flight on his side of Wabash Avenue. She was one block ahead. At Van Buren, she turned. Two thoughts ran through Alfano's head: one, that's where she'd parked, and two, Van Buren 'L' station. His years said the 'L.' The traffic was too thick for her to get anywhere by car, whereas if she made it to the station and a train, she could go anywhere before he could stop her.

Alfano's heart was pounding; his pack a day of cigarettes didn't help. Breathing hard, he spotted her amidst a crowd of late-evening revelers. She briefly stopped at the corner of State Street before lunging into the cross traffic. She saw him too and sprinted for the station entry.

As Alfano dodged his way through the honking horns and chrome bumpers on State Street, he was baffled to see three men jump from the shadows and grab Acerbi. She twisted out of their grip. They were yelling something he couldn't hear over the traffic; she yelled back, then elevated the Luger and fired at one of the attackers. The man clutched his gut and fell. The other two men backed away, seemingly stunned.

Alfano raised his weapon and fired; the bullet pinged loudly off the steel support structure of the overhead tracks. Acerbi whirled toward him, her gauzy gown swirling around her long legs. She looked almost like a dancer doing a pirouette. She steadied herself and raised her weapon again.

As the crowd on Van Buren screamed and ran for cover, Alfano dropped to one knee, took a deep breath and with a steady hand fired once more. She again spun on her heels. This time blood appeared on the green dress a finger width above her left breast. She plucked at the tear; blood leaked onto her hands and the pistol she still held. As if a life switch had been pulled, the pistol tumbled into the folds of the dress and Carla Acerbi dropped into its billowing fabric.

34

ALFANO paced in the lobby of the mayor's office. Three crushed cigarettes lay in the ashtray now adorning the low table in front of a large leather couch. After personally retrieving the ashtray from the receptionist's bottom desk drawer, each time he lit a cigarette, he incurred the wrath of the woman sitting behind the desk. The secretary cleared her throat and coughed, making a weird and scratchy sound. Alfano thought she'd learned it from strangling cats. He checked his watch again; he'd been waiting for thirty minutes. He could think of a dozen places he wanted to be right now, and none of them was here.

Balbo and his squadron had left Chicago two days earlier and were now being feted in New York City and Washington D.C. Even President Roosevelt had gotten into the act with a special reception for the general. For his part, Alfano was glad to be rid of the visitors.

The body of Carla Acerbi, alias Donna Delucca, lay on a marble slab in Dr. Abrahamson's morgue with one forty-five caliber hole through her heart—a heart that had never really functioned like the other billions of hearts in the world. The coroner confided that there was some justice in the world; Acerbi's body now lay on the same slab as her first victim,

Mary Ann DeAngelo.

They'd found Acerbi's Oldsmobile a few hundred feet from where she'd taken her last breath. Through the vehicle's registration, they tracked the car to Acerbi's apartment—the same apartment that the police had forcibly entered a few hours after Acerbi left it for the last time. Aside from Acerbi's final encounter with Alfano, police had meanwhile located her Chicago residence, aided by the license plate number the tough kids from the Cavallo murder location had given Alfano. Acerbi's landlord had been more than willing to show police the lease agreement. McDunnah was not too surprised to learn that the apartment had been leased to the Italian government, whose local officials denied knowledge of Acerbi's presence or activities. Guido Barbieri's signature was all over the document; he had just left on ocean liner *Rex* to return to Italy. With no response from the Italian consulate, McDunnah sought the help of the FBI and learned that someone who looked a lot like Carla Acerbi had arrived in New York City one month earlier, traveling under the name Juliana Provensa. The Italian government had not yet responded to inquiries about the identity or whereabouts of Miss Provensa. As far as Alfano was concerned or cared, he'd taken one very nasty bitch off his streets.

The trio who'd rushed Acerbi as she fled from Alfano had nothing to do with government or police. When the men were detained and questioned, two of them testified that Acerbi had assaulted Herman a few hours earlier and Herman had not appreciated the beating. Upon seeing her again, he'd wanted revenge. The bullet she'd fired at him had passed through his abdomen, but he would survive.

Two drawers over from the body of Carla Acerbi (the name written on the toe tag), lay the body of Matteo Cavallo. His family in Italy had been notified, although the disposition of his remains was uncertain. Alfano contacted the local archdiocese to see if church officials could help with the burial, but there had not been a final determination. Since it was rumored that Cavallo had been trying to kill General Balbo—an unsubstantiated story that somehow grabbed the media headlines—no one was sure about the response from the government in Rome.

Sal Rizzo was sitting in a Miami jail, awaiting extradition to Chicago. He'd been apprehended as he got off the *Royal Palm Streamliner* in Miami with a steamship ticket to Lisbon in his pocket. Alfano wasn't sure if it was worth all the effort. Rizzo would be charged with stealing the *Blackhawk* and maybe something to do with damaging the Michigan Avenue Bridge. The feds were pondering other charges, including conspiracy to commit murder. Since there were no witnesses, a conviction would be hard.

Maria DeRosa was out on bail; her parents had posted a bond, using their restaurant as collateral. She'd been charged with aiding and abetting the theft of the boat—which she totally denied knowing anything about. The feds were trying to get her to turn on Lucca Barone. Alfano had seen that one before; she would never turn on the love of her life. He'd also heard that Nardo, DeRosa's boss at the Italian Pavilion, had fired her for not showing up to work. Bitch.

Lucca Barone, son of a wealthy Rome banker, cooled *his* heels and butt in a Cook County jail, waiting for whatever would befall him. At the behest of the Chicago attorney hired by the Barone family, Lucca denied knowing anything about the boat, Rizzo, Cavallo, or General Balbo. Alfano knew the attorney quite well. The mouthpiece had defended many from the Outfit and the mobs around Chicago; one Alphonse Capone had been a source of many billable hours. McDunnah said that the chances of Barone going to prison were as good as a Chicago politician getting into heaven.

At last, the mahogany door to the mayor's office opened.

Standing in the entry was His Honor himself, resplendent in a new suit and sharp tie. Behind him stood Patrick Nash. Alfano looked for strings and, even knowing they were there, didn't see any.

"Detective Anthony Alfano, my favorite, and the city's most famous and righteous man of the hour," said the mayor. "Come in, Tony. Come in. We certainly missed you the other night at dinner; they tell me you were out saving our great Italian friend and our World's Fair as well. Tell me all about it."

THE END

ACKNOWLEDGEMENTS

As a self-published author I want to thank a few people for their work, directly and indirectly, in the production of this story. To Cheryl R. Ganz and her book, *The 1933 Chicago World's Fair, A Century of Progress*. It is an excellent work on the background, construction, and development of the fair. The Century of Progress fair was one of the major reasons why Chicago, in the midst of the Depression, was able to weather the tough economic trouble that plagued America through the 1930s. Her book describes this effort brilliantly. Surprisingly, there is a dearth of written works about this important event that spanned two years. I believe that it should be studied more.

During the past few years the venerable *Chicago Tribune* has digitized their morning edition of the paper, it is available on-line. These digital issues cover the years from 1841-1991. *Chicago Jazz* relies on the day-to-day events as reported for 1933 in Chicago as written in this newspaper. I also want to acknowledge the dozens of old newsreels of the fair that have been digitized and placed on YouTube and other platforms. It is interesting to note that the entire trip of Italo Balbo and his squadron, from Italy to the United States and their return to Italy, are also available through digitized newsreel footage.

Most especially I want to acknowledge two people who reviewed the final manuscript. First to Bonnie Randall, my wife and muse, for her help in working out the story and giving it a thorough first edit. And to my editor, Laurel Leigh, for her help making the final manuscript the best it could be.

Any errors and typos (hopefully few and far between) are mine.

April, 2016

Reviews Please

Today authors rely heavily on the reviews posted by our readers. As an independent self-publisher this is even more important than traditionally published books. If you have enjoyed this book, please take a few minutes and post a review on Goodreads and Amazon.

About the Author

Gregory C. Randall

Mr. Randall is Michigan born, Chicago raised and Californian by choice. He makes his home in Walnut Creek, California.

Mr. Randall is the author of fiction and non-fiction works available through the usual outlets and the Windsor Hill Publishing website.

For more on future Tony Alfano thrillers and information the Sharon O'Mara Chronicles and planned sequels, please visit and connect with Greg online:

http://www.gregorycrandall.com
http://www.gregorycrandall.info
Read his blog:
http://www.writing4death.blogspot.com

Other books by Mr. Randall available both in print and as ebooks:

Fiction
Elk River

The Tony Alfano Thrillers
Chicago Swing
Chicago Jazz

The Sharon O'Mara Chronicles
Land Swap For Death
Containers For Death
Toulouse For Death
12th Man For Death
Diamonds For Death

Non-fiction
America's Original GI Town, Park Forest, Illinois

These books can be purchased in paperback through all bookstores.

I hope you enjoyed this story!

www.ingramcontent.com/pod-product-compliance
Lightning Source LLC
Chambersburg PA
CBHW030107260626
47156CB00008B/2558